All Those English Love Songs

都是愛情惹的英文歌

李音・戴衛平・劉墐
主編

非凡出版

前 言

《都是愛情惹的英文歌》選輯不同風格的英文歌曲，涵蓋流行、藍調、搖滾、鄉村、爵士、民謠等大眾熟知的曲風類型，為讀者呈現一個色彩斑斕的音樂世界。

本書編者對近 100 首風靡全球的經典英文歌曲進行了翻譯與深度解析，通過重釋經典佳作，為讀者開啟全新的英語學習之門，以求帶給廣大英語愛好者更為原汁原味的文化體驗。同時，作為經典英文歌曲的集萃，本書也希望能給所有熱愛音樂、追求時尚的歌迷們，打造一場聽覺盛宴。

之所以選擇經典英文歌曲的歌詞作為文化輸入的媒介，其一是考慮到歌曲的特質：其本身就具有無形的感染力與滲透性，是最為生動有趣的語言表達形式，能夠輕鬆將英語學習者帶入異域文化的深層次體驗中；其二，

歌詞有別於其他文學載體，它們藝術氣息濃郁、感情豐富真摯卻又甚少拘泥於語言形式，是不可多得的地道英語學習文本。以最活潑的方式學習最純正的英語表達，能使我們對語言學習達到事半功倍的效果；其三，既為經典，大家便會對其中很多歌詞津津樂道，而我們對詞曲背後的深意是否能夠繞開理解誤區？對經典的珍藏是否能夠在心中永恆定格？本書通過對歌曲多角度的剖析解答，力求幫助讀者快速、準確地掌握這些經典歌曲的理解。

我們對對於歌曲的解析，劃分為四道風景線：一、導語部分，概述該曲的背景知識及其歌手的音樂成就，幫助讀者對所喜愛的經典歌曲和歌手形象獲取較為完整的認知；二、英文歌詞與中文歌詞兩部分對照呈現，在展示原作風采的同時，希望編者所譯的中文歌詞能作為眾多英語愛好者學習、研究詞作的一塊點金之石；

三、註釋部分，是對歌詞中出現的不常見詞彙的註解，使讀者在輕鬆享受歌曲的同時，掌握更多生僻詞彙或常見詞的多重意義；四、設置了對精彩之處深入解密的特色環節，幫助大家對歌詞中出現的難懂或不常見詞彙、習語、俚語，以及具有特殊句子結構或特定文化內涵的知識進行詳細解釋，以便讀者理解原文，並掌握更多英語知識，達到舉一反三的目的。

相對於同類書籍而言，本書最大的特色是通過對精選的經典歌詞從語法知識、文化常識等方面，進行整合解析，為廣大英語、音樂愛好者構築了學習原汁原味英語的最佳模式與快速通道。為了更好地感受歌曲的魅力，廣大讀者可在相關音樂網站自行下載歌曲，親耳聆聽歌者們的精彩演唱，感受其地道發音。

我們深知本書的編寫不可能面面俱到、完美無瑕，對於英語語言的學習和研究也只是冰山一隅。在編寫中，我們忠實秉承文化傳播者的職責，竭力做到客觀、準確重現英語文化的精美之貌，不求提升各方學術造詣，只求為英語學習者打開一扇異域風情之窗，使讀者可以循序漸進地融入正宗的語言環境，直觀地領略歐美人文情懷。由於篇幅有限，編者將有些歌詞太長的歌曲進行了副歌部分的刪減，望廣大讀者予以理解，疏漏之處，望廣大讀者不吝賜教。

$\mathcal{C}$ontents

目　錄

Contents

目 錄

Adele, Bob Dylan, The Bea

Michael Jackso

ic Clapton, Jason Mraz, Joan Baez, Oasis……

ah Jones, Queen, U2……

Almost Lover
無緣戀人

A FINE FRENZY
ONE CELL IN THE SEA

英文
歌詞

Your **fingertips** across my skin
The palm trees **swaying** in the wind in my chase
You sang me Spanish **lullabies**
The sweetest sadness in your eyes
Clever trick
I never wanna see you unhappy
I thought you want the same for me

Goodbye my almost lover
Goodbye my hopeless dream
I'm trying not to think about you
Can't you just let me be
So long my luckless romance
My back is turned on you
Should've known you'd bring me heartbreak
Almost lovers always do

We walked along a crowded street
You took my hand and danced with me in the shade
And when you left you kissed my lips
You told me you'd never ever forget these images

I cannot go to the ocean
I cannot try the streets at night
I cannot wake up in the morning
Without you on my mind
So you're gonna and I'm **haunted**
And I bet you are just fine
Did I make it that easy
To walk right in and out of my life

詞彙
註釋

fingertip *n.* 指尖

sway *v.* 擺動

lullaby *n.* 搖籃曲

haunted *adj.* 煩惱的

A Fine Frenzy 是一位極富音樂天賦的歌手，這歌是她 18 歲時有感而發所創作的一首另類搖滾歌曲。這首戀愛挽歌在歐洲引起強烈反響，被 MTV「真人騷」節目 *The Hills* 以及知名電視劇 *Big Shots* 選作配樂。

 中文譯文

你用指尖把我輕輕撫摸
棕櫚樹葉在風中盡情婆娑
你輕輕哼着那熟悉的搖籃曲
目光中流淌着甜蜜的痛楚
這只是騙局
我願你快樂不止
我以為你願我也如此

永別吧，我的無緣戀人
永別吧，我無緣的夢痕
我會努力把你遺忘
就讓我獨自這樣
永別吧，我無緣的愛戀
我要轉身忘記一切
早該知道你會給我無盡心傷
無緣戀人都是這樣

我們曾穿過擁擠的街道
牽手共舞在林蔭大道
別時你給我一個輕吻
說着你不會忘記這一幕幕

再也沒有海邊浪漫的感覺
再也不能漫步在子夜的街
即使是在夢裏
你也在我腦海裏
你已離去，我心中卻滿是煩惱
但願你一切都安好
我會好好的
你是我人生中的匆匆過客

（李娟 譯）

 精彩之處

sweetest sadness：這裏使用了矛盾修辭法，表現了主人翁悲欣交集的心情。

I cannot：歌曲中 I cannot 的連用突出了美好過往的難以忘懷，與現在孑然一身的淒清形成強烈對比。cannot 處的重音更表明想要忘記以往是自欺欺人，那根植於腦海中的昔日，只能讓人更加痛苦。

Hometown Glory
故 鄉 的 榮 耀

I've been walking in the same way as I did
Missing out the cracks in the pavement
And **tutting** my heel and **strutting** my feet
"Is there anything I can do for you dear ?
Is there anyone I could call ? "
"No and thank you, please Madam
I ain't lost, just wandering"

Round my hometown
Memories are fresh
Round my hometown
Ooh the people I've met
Are the wonders of my world

I like it in the city
When the air is so thick and **opaque**
I love to see everybody
In short skirts, shorts and shades
I like it in the city when two worlds **collide**
You get the people and the government
Everybody taking different sides

Shows that we aren't gonna stand shit
Shows that we are united
Shows that we aren't gonna take it

詞彙
註釋

tut *v.* 發嘖嘖聲

strut *v.* 在……上趾高
氣揚地走

opaque *adj.* 不透明
的

collide *v.* 碰撞

這是阿黛爾（Adele）個人第一支單曲。阿黛爾因其渾厚、富有磁性的嗓音漸漸走紅。她用自己樸實的情感完美地演繹了這首略帶傷感和失落的歌曲。沉浸在阿黛爾的歌聲中，你會有種靈魂深處的震撼。耐人回味的歌詞，打動心靈的旋律，會讓你對阿黛爾的歌聲欲罷不能。

中文譯文

我一直用同樣的方式行走
錯過人行道上的紋縫
鞋跟嗒嗒作響，我闊步走着
「有甚麼需要幫忙的嗎？
有甚麼人我可以聯繫嗎？」
「不用了，謝謝你，夫人
我沒有迷路，只是在閒逛」

繞着我的故鄉
記憶猶新
繞着我的故鄉
我看見的人們
是我生命中的奇跡

我愛這個季節的城市
濃重的空氣顯得不透明
我喜歡看着人們
在樹蔭下穿着短裙，短褲
我愛這樣的城市，兩種世界碰撞中
誕生了民族與政府
人人可以持不同的立場

我們不會逆來順受
我們團結一致
我們不會隨便接受

（葛婷婷　譯）

精彩之處

And...feet： tut 和 strut 這兩個動詞繪聲繪色地將主人翁走路的姿態表現出來，同時兩個動詞的尾音相同，後面接的名詞也具有相同音節，極具音律感。

everybody taking different sides： 這是本歌詞中的昇華之筆，主人翁對自己的故鄉熱愛之情在此得到凝聚。故鄉的民主氣息，故鄉人民的團結與積極讓她深深地愛上了這片土地。同時後面三小句歌詞最後一個單詞的尾音相同，增強了歌曲的節奏感。

► N O W P L A Y I N G

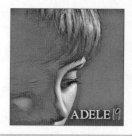

ADELE 19

Make You Feel My Love
讓 你 感 受 我 的 愛

英文
歌詞

When the rain is blowing in your face

And the whole world is on your case

I could offer you a warm embrace

To make you feel my love

When the evening shadows and the stars appear

And there is no one there to dry your tears

I could hold you for a million years

To make you feel my love

I know you haven't **made your mind up** yet

But I would never **do you wrong**

I've known it from the moment that we met

No doubt in my mind where you belong

I'd go hungry, I'd go black and blue

I'd go crawling down the avenue

No, there's nothing that I wouldn't do

To make you feel my love

The storms are raging on the rolling sea

And on the highway of regret

Though winds of change are throwing wild and free

You ain't seen nothing like me yet

I could make you happy, make your dreams come true

Nothing that I wouldn't do

Go to the ends of the Earth for you

To make you feel my love

詞彙
註釋

make up one's mind
下定決心

**do sb. wrong 傷害某
人**

翻唱自美國唱作人 Bob Dylan 的作品，此歌收錄於阿黛爾 2008 年發行的首張專輯《19》中，該專輯獲得水星音樂獎提名，並在英國專輯排行榜上得到第一名佳績，全球超過 700 萬的銷售量。作為翻唱最成功的版本之一，這首歌多次被選在電視劇中播出。

當雨水不斷擊打着你的臉頰
當整個世界都對你發出惡言
我會將你擁入我溫暖的胸懷
讓你感受到我對你的愛
當夜幕拉開，星空出現
卻無人為你擦乾淚水
我會將你抱住，直到永遠
讓你感受到我對你的愛

我知道你尚未做出抉擇
我願靜靜等待那個抉擇
在我們相遇的那一刻
我就深深體會到這一點
你一定會佔據我的腦海
為了你我願意挨餓受苦
我願意忍受各種煎熬
沒有甚麼能夠將我阻撓
讓你感受到我對你的愛

人生就像波濤洶湧的大海
難免會留下些許遺憾
儘管生活中常卷起無常的風
但我愛你的心永遠不變
我會讓你開心，我會幫你圓夢
我將盡我所能
陪你走到世界盡頭
讓你感受到我對你的愛

（王晶　譯）

精彩之處

black and blue： 固定搭配，意為「遍體鱗傷，青一塊紫一塊」。英語中很多包含顏色的短語在譯成中文時要注意。比如：black tea（紅茶），feel blue（心情低落），greenback（美元）。

The storms...free： 作者運用隱喻，把人生比作大海，把生活中不如意的事比作無常的大風，非常形象地展現了生活的艱辛，但是這些艱難卻阻擋不了作者對愛人的愛。

Someone like You
某 人 如 你

I heard that you settled down
That you found a girl and you married now
I heard that your dreams came true
Guess she gave you things, I didn't give to you
Old friend, why are you so shy
It ain't like you to hold back or hide from the lie
I hate to **turn up** out of the blue uninvited
But I couldn't stay away, I couldn't fight it
I'd hoped you'd see my face &
that you'd be reminded
That for me, it isn't over

Never mind, I'll find someone like you
I wish nothing but the best, for you too
Don't forget me, I beg, I remember you said
Sometimes it lasts in love
but sometimes it hurts instead
Sometimes it lasts in love but sometimes it hurts
instead, yeah

You know, how the time flies
Only yesterday, was the time of our lives
We were born and raised in a summer **haze**
Bound by the surprise of our glory days

Nothing compares, no worries or cares
Regrets and mistakes they're memories made
Who would have known how bittersweet this
would taste

**詞彙
註釋**

turn up 出現

haze *n.* 薄霧

bind *v.* 結合

這首歌收錄於阿黛爾（Adele）的第二張個人錄音室專輯《21》中，該單曲在 2011 年公告牌（Billboard）排行榜中奪得五週單曲冠軍，並且是公告牌史上第一支只有鋼琴而無其他樂器伴奏的單曲冠軍。2012 年第 54 屆格林美頒獎晚會上，阿黛爾憑藉該單曲獲得年度最佳新人和最佳流行歌手。

中文譯文

聽說，你已安定下來了
遇到了她並且已結婚了
聽說，你的夢想成真了
我猜她給了你我不曾給你的東西
老朋友，為甚麼這麼害羞呢
猶豫不決，遮遮掩掩，這可一點都不像你哦
我討厭未被邀請卻不請自來
但是我卻這樣遠離你，也無力抗爭
我希望你能看清我的臉，
好好記住
對我來說，結束並沒有那麼容易

沒關係啊，我會遇到一個像你一樣的愛人
對你，我只有真心祝福，別無他求
不要忘記我，我懇求你，我記得你曾經說過
有時候愛情是永恆的，
但有時又是如此讓人心痛
有時候愛情是永恆的，但有時又是如此讓人
傷心，的確如此

你應該知道，時光已經流逝
只有昨天才是我們在一起的回憶
我們的愛在夏日的薄霧中成長
那些青春歲月承載着驚喜與輝煌

沒人能夠與你相提並論，無人擔心，無人在意
記憶裏滿是悔恨和錯誤
又有誰知曉這其中的
酸甜苦辣呢

（任欣 譯）

精彩之處

Sometimes...yeah： 這是一個對比句。but 一詞連接了 last 和 hurt，強烈對比顯現出愛情的兩面性，有溫暖又伴隨着疼痛。

Only yesterday...lives：
這是一個倒裝句，目的是為了強調語氣，更生動地表達出舊日的幸福時光已是過往。

Goodbye
再見

I can see the pain living in your eyes
And I know how hard you try
You **deserve** to have so much more
I can feel your heart and I **sympathize**
And I'll never criticize all you've ever meant to my life

I don't want to **let you down**
I don't want to lead you on
I don't want to hold you back
From where you might belong

You would never ask me why
My heart is so disguised
I just can't live a lie anymore
I would rather hurt myself
Than to ever make you cry
There's nothing left to say but good-bye

You deserve the chance at the kind of love
I'm not sure I'm worthy of
Losing you is painful to me

You would never ask me why
My heart is so **disguised**
I just can't live a lie anymore
I would rather hurt myself
Than to ever make you cry
There's nothing left to try now
It's gonna hurt us both
It's no other way than to say goodbye

詞彙 註釋

deserve *v.* 應得

sympathize *v.* 憐憫

let sb. down 讓人失望

disguised *adj.* 偽裝的

空中補給合唱團（Air Supply）不斷地創造出絕美而出色的流行歌曲，並因此而在他們長達 20 多年的音樂旅程中一再地改寫排行榜歷史，幾乎每首歌都曾在歐美各大流行音樂排行榜上佔據過位置。情感純粹、音樂簡潔、旋律抒情優美是該合唱團最大的特點。

 中文譯文

我能夠看到你眼中的痛苦
我知道你努力嘗試了
你應該得到這些
我感同身受，心有憐憫
我將絕不評判你對我生命的意義

我不想讓你失望
我不想帶你走
我不想挽回你
從你所屬的地方

你從不問我原因
我內心充滿矯飾
我不能再活在謊言中
我寧願傷害自己
也不願讓你哭泣
我們只能說再見

你該擁有愛的機會
我不確定自己是否值得
失去你，我很痛苦

你從不問我原因
我內心充滿矯飾
我不能再活在謊言中
我寧願傷害自己
也不願讓你哭泣
現在已沒有機會可以再試了
這將會傷害我們
除了說再見，已別無他路了

（壽業寧　譯）

 精彩之處

deserve to：表達了作者對對方的理解。

And I'll...life：criticize 是評判的意思，後面跟的是賓語從句，這裏表現了對方對作者生命的重要意義。

I would...cry：would rather...than... 是「寧願……也不願意……」，這句話表達了作者對對方的愛之深。

歌中 eye、try、goodbye、why 以及 cry 等兩兩押韻，雙母音 [ai] 發音飽滿到位，底氣十足，給聽眾帶來強烈的震撼。

Amanda Seyfried

Little House
歡 樂 的 小 屋

I love this place
But it's <u>haunted</u> without you
My tired heart is beating so slow
<u>Our hearts sing less than we wanted</u>
We wanted our hearts sing 'cause
We do not know, we do not know
To light the night
To help us grow, to help us grow
It is not said, i always know

You can catch me
Don't you run, don't you run
If you live another day
In this happy little house
The fire's here to stay

To light the night
To help us grow, to help us grow
It is not said, i always know

Please don't **make a fuss**
It won't go away
The wonder of it all
The wonder that I made
I am here to stay
I am here to stay
Stay

**❚❚ 詞彙
註釋**

make a fuss 大驚小
怪

艾曼達·塞弗里德（Amanda Seyfried）因出演 *Jennifer's Body*、*Mamma Mia!* 等片為人關注。2008 年入選 Independent Critics 網站評比的「全球百張最漂亮臉蛋」，排名第 46。這首歌是她在電影《分手的情書》（*Dear John*）中所唱的插曲和片尾曲，歌曲悠揚、輕靈，充滿了對愛人的思戀，以及對愛情的感悟和因時間而沉澱的愛所帶來的成長。

中文譯文

我喜歡這裏
但是我有點迷惑，因為這沒有了你
我的心累了，跳動慢了
有許多的話語，我們的心無法訴說
我們渴望互相傾訴，因為
我們不知道，我們不知道
讓黑夜不再黑暗
讓我們成長，讓我們長大
這並不代表，我一直都懂

你要抓緊我
不要離開，不要離開
如果你能再生活一天
在這歡樂的小屋
愛的火焰就會繼續

讓黑夜不再黑暗
讓我們成長，讓我們長大
這並不代表，我一直都懂

請不要驚奇
它不會消失
它帶來的驚奇
我留下的奇跡
我會留在這裏
我會留在這裏
在這裏

（邊雪寧 譯）

精彩之處

haunted：原意是「鬧鬼的，縈繞不去的」。而這裏表示「你」離開之後，這個地方就讓我觸景傷情，讓我害怕沒有「你」的這個地方。

Our hearts sing less than we wanted：「你」走之後我才發現，有很多想說的話彼此都沒有說出口。

Andy Williams

Love Story
愛情故事

英文歌詞

Where do I begin to tell the story
Of how great a love can be
The sweet love story
That is older than the sea
The simple truth about the love, she brings to me
Where do I start

With her first hello
She gave a meaning, to this empty world of mine
There'll never be another love
Another time
She came into my life
And made the living fine
She fills my heart

She fills my heart
With very special things
With angel songs
With **wild** imaginings
She fills my soul with so much love
That anywhere I go I'm never lonely
With her along, who could be lonely
I reach for her hand
It's always there

How long does it last
Can love be **measured**, by the hours in a day
I have no answers now
But this much I can say
I know I'll need her
Till the stars all **burn away**
And she'll be there

詞彙 註釋

wild *adj.* 狂熱的

measure *v.* 衡量

burn away 燃盡

這首歌的演唱者為享譽全球的美國歌壇大師安迪·威廉斯（Andy Williams）。美國前總統列根曾讚譽威廉斯的聲音是「國寶」。《愛情故事》（Love Story）這部電影曾獲 7 項奧斯卡獎提名，並最終獲得最佳原創音樂獎。該曲作為電影的主題曲貫穿全片，旋律優美動聽，歌詞真摯感人。

中文譯文

我該從何講起
這偉大的愛情故事
這甜蜜的愛情故事
比大海還古老
她給我帶來了愛情的真諦
我該從何說起

她的第一聲問候
使我空虛的世界變得有意義
再也不會有另一個愛人
沒有另一次
她走入我的生命
使我生活變得精彩
她充滿我心房

她充滿我心房
帶給我奇妙的感覺
天使般的歌聲
和狂野的想像
她用無盡的愛充滿我心靈
無論走到哪裏，我都不會感到寂寞
與她在一起，誰還會孤單
我去拉她的手
它總在那裏等候

愛情能持續多久
愛可以用小時來衡量嗎
我現在沒有答案
但我可以說這麼多
我需要她
直到群星燃盡
而她也將在那裏

精彩之處

I have...say：這一句後半部分用的是倒裝語序，把本應作 say 賓語的 this much 前置，為的是把 say 放在句尾和前句的 day 押韻。

Till the stars all burn away：這句話的意思等同於 till the end of the world，stars burn away 本意是「星體燃盡」，在這裏表達「萬物毀滅，愛情仍永存」的道理。在中外詩歌中也經常出現這樣的修辭，比如 I'll love you till the sea go dry, till the rocks melt away.（我會永遠愛你，直到海枯石爛。）

（李音 譯）

The Thrill Is Gone
激 情 已 逝

英文
歌詞

The **thrill** is gone
The thrill is gone away
The thrill is gone, baby
The thrill is gone away
You know you've done me wrong, baby
And you'll be sorry someday

The thrill is gone
The thrill has gone away from me
The thrill is gone, baby
The thrill has gone away from me
Although I'll still living
But so lonely I'll be

The thrill is gone
It's gone away for good
Oh, The thrill is gone
It's gone away for good
Some day I know I'll be open armed, baby
Just like I know a man should

You know I'm free, free now baby
I'm free from your **spell**
Well I'm free, free, free now
I'm free from your spell
And now that it's all over
All I can do is wish you well

**⏸ 詞彙
註釋**

thrill *n.* 激情

spell *n.* 魔力

這首歌是比·比·金（B. B. King）不可多得的佳作之一。作為藍調音樂王國的主宰，這位美國黑人歌手發行過 50 多張膾炙人口的經典專輯，榮列藍調名人堂與搖滾名人堂，並獲格林美「終生成就獎」。美國前總統喬治布殊親自為其頒發了美國最高國民榮譽獎「總統自由勳章」。

中文譯文

激情已不在
激情已遠去
親愛的，我們之間再無激情
激情永逝
你確實冤枉了我
或有一天，你會歉疚

激情已不在
我的激情，枯萎凋零
親愛的，我們彼此已非熱戀
我的生活，行屍走肉
歲月依舊
人如孤魂

激情已不在
永無重燃日
親愛的，我們從此波瀾不驚
激情永逝
有朝一日，我終將釋懷
男兒志在四方

孑然一身，不困於情
不再為你癡狂
無拘無束
不再為你癡狂
萬事皆塵埃落定
唯願你歲月靜好

（趙瑋 譯）

精彩之處

for good：常用於表達「一勞永逸地」，即「一經發生，永成定局」的意思。面對愛情無疾而終，男主角更多的是看穿現實，不願委曲求全。

Some day...should：open armed 多指張開雙臂熱情歡迎，而若結合後半句，應理解為「釋懷」之意。整句的點睛之筆在於，作詞人用最簡單的詞語 a man should 表現出了最厚重的沉澱：男兒當心胸開闊，志在四方，不耿耿於懷，不一蹶不振。

free from your spell：spell 在此為「魅力、魔力」之意。free from 指不再為曾經的愛人無力自拔，對她的癡迷與眷戀在逐漸淡失，也是主人翁對自己今後生活狀態的一種期許。

Raindrops Keep Falling on My Head
雨點不斷落在我頭上

Raindrops keep falling on my head
And just like the guy whose feet are too big for his bed
Nothin' seems to fit
Those raindrops are falling on my head they keep falling

So I just did me some talkin' to the sun
And I said I didn't like the way he got things done
Sleepin' on the job
Those raindrops are falling on my head they keep falling

But there's one thing I know
The **blues** they send to meet me won't **defeat** me
It won't be long till happiness steps up to greet me

Raindrops keep falling on my head
But that doesn't mean my eyes will soon be turnin' red
Crying's not for me
'Cause I'm never gonna stop the rain by **complaining**
Because I'm free
Nothing's worrying me

詞彙
註釋

blue *n.* 憂愁

defeat *v.* 擊敗

complain *v.* 抱怨

這首流行搖滾歌曲是 B·J·湯瑪斯（B. J. Thomas）的代表作，為電影《神槍手與智多星》（*Butch Cassidy and the Sundance Kid*）的插曲，該曲曾獲最佳電影原創歌曲獎。湯瑪斯也曾 5 次獲得格林美獎。此曲曾被多次翻唱，其中 1995 年威爾斯樂隊 Manic Streer Preachers 重新灌錄這歌，收錄於雜錦大碟 *Help* 中，為戰難兒童籌款。

中文譯文

雨點不斷落在我頭上
像一個小床躺了一個大個子
一點都不合適
雨點還在不斷落在我頭上

所以我只好去告訴太陽
我不喜歡他那樣做
工作時間睡覺
雨點還在不斷落在我頭上

但是有一件事我知道
它們帶來的憂鬱不會擊敗我
幸福不久就會到來

雨點不斷落在我頭上
但那並不代表我會紅了眼眶
我不哭
因為我從不用抱怨讓天放晴
因為我自由自在
無憂無慮

（邊雪寧 譯）

精彩之處

nothin'、talkin'、sleepin'、turnin'： 本篇歌詞中有很多 -ing 寫成 in'，這在歌詞中十分常見，這樣縮寫能夠縮短音長，加快節奏，而且去掉 g 後，in 和後面的母音單詞可以連讀，這樣英文歌詞能夠唱得更連貫協調。Rap 中尤為常用。

歌曲旋律優美，節奏歡快，具有跳躍感，使聽眾彷彿置身於滴答的小雨中。歌詞中 head、bed 和 red 押韻，me 和 free 押韻，發音急促有力，在句尾戛然而止，增強節奏感，同時為歌曲增添幾分俏皮感。

The Beatles

▶ N O W   P L A Y I N G

Hey Jude
嘿，裘德

英文
歌詞

Hey Jude, don't make it bad
Take a sad song and make it better
Remember, to let her into your heart
Then you can start to make it better

Hey Jude, don't be afraid
You **were made to** go out and get her
The minute you let her under your skin
Then you begin to make it better

And anytime you feel the pain
Hey Jude, **refrain**
Don't carry the world upon your shoulder
For well you know that it's a fool
Who plays it cool
By making his world a little colder

Hey Jude, don't let me down
You have found her now go and get her
Remember (Hey Jude) to let her into your heart
Then you can start to make it better

So let it out and let it in
Hey Jude, begin
You're waiting for someone to perform with
Don't you know that it's just you
Hey Jude, you'll do
The movement you need is on your shoulder

⏸ 詞彙
註釋

be made to 此處意為
「註定」

refrain *v.* 忍耐

這首輕柔搖滾歌曲由披頭四（The Beatles）成員保羅·麥卡特尼（Paul McCartney）創作，發行於 1968 年。當時，樂隊另一成員約翰·連儂與前妻的婚姻走到了盡頭，而保羅一直以來非常喜愛約翰當時 5 歲的兒子，他擔心大人之間的婚變會對孩子帶來心理上的陰影，於是通過創作這首歌來給予他安慰和鼓勵。

 中文譯文

嘿，裘德！別消沉
唱首悲傷的歌，振作起來
記得真心愛她
開始新的美好生活

嘿，裘德！別擔心
你註定會去追逐她，擁有她
把她融入心底的那一刻
開始新的美好生活

無論何時你感到痛苦
嘿，裘德！要放鬆
別把一切都自己扛
你知道愚蠢的人
才故作瀟灑
把自己的世界偽裝得冷酷

嘿，裘德！別讓我失望
既已找到她就要勇敢追求
記得（嘿，裘德！）真心愛她
才能開始新的美好生活

所以，放下過去繼續愛
嘿，裘德！開始吧
你期待有人和你一同演繹人生
要知道你才是主角
嘿，裘德！你能行
未來在自己手中

（喬楠 譯）

 精彩之處

在 2012 年倫敦奧運會開幕式上，作為壓軸演出的保羅再一次演唱了這首歌曲，向世界傳達了和平、團結、友善的精神。

let her into your heart：
直譯過來是「讓她進入你心裏」，其實是「把她放在心裏，用心去愛她」的意思。

under the skin： 是「在心裏」的意思，放在句中可說成是「融入心底」。

The Beatles

Let It Be
順 其 自 然

When I find myself in times of trouble
Mother Mary comes to me
Speaking words of wisdom, let it be
And in my hour of darkness
She is standing right in front of me
Speaking words of wisdom, let it be

Let it be, let it be
Whisper words of wisdom, let it be

And when the broken hearted people
Living in the world agree
There will be an answer, let it be
For though they may be parted
There is still a chance that they will see
There will be an answer, let it be

Let it be, let it be
Yeah there will be an answer, let it be
Let it be, let it be
Whisper words of wisdom, let it be

And when the night is cloudy
There is still a light that shines on me
Shine on until tomorrow, let it be
I wake up to the sound of music
Mother Mary comes to me
Speaking words of wisdom, let it be
Yeah let it be, let it be
Oh there will be an answer, let it be

這首歌出自英國搖滾樂隊披頭四（The Beatles）第 12 張專輯《順其自然》（*Let It Be*），發行於 1970 年，該專輯獲第十三屆格林美最佳原創電影電視音樂獎。披頭四在英國一共發行了 12 張錄音室專輯，到目前為止，該樂隊在美國共售出 1.77 億張唱片，成為歷史上銷量最高的樂隊。1965 年，披頭四獲英國女王伊莉莎白二世頒發不列顛帝國勳章。

中文譯文

當我在困境中迷茫
聖母瑪利亞來到我身旁
訴說人生真諦，順其自然
當我在黑暗中彷徨
她就站在我面前
訴說人生真諦，順其自然

順其自然，順其自然
輕聲訴說人生真諦，順其自然

當傷心的人兒
相惜相伴
一切終會有答案，順其自然
因為即使別離
終將有一日再相見
一切終會有答案，順其自然

順其自然，順其自然
哦，一切終會有答案，順其自然
順其自然，順其自然
輕聲訴說人生的真諦，順其自然

陰雲遮月的夜晚
仍有一束光照耀我
照耀着直到天明，順其自然
酣夢初醒，樂聲蕩漾
聖母瑪利亞來到我身旁
訴說人生真諦，順其自然
順其自然，順其自然
哦，一切終會有答案，順其自然

（祝佳琦 譯）

精彩之處

Mother Mary：聖母瑪利亞，英文名為 Blessed Virgin Mary，是《聖經·新約》中耶穌的母親。

let it be：順其自然，此句表達的是一種無奈、隨性的狀態，暗指一種坦然的生活態度，不必處處計較，順其自然即可。

歌詞中有多處 [i] 的尾韻，如 me、be、agree、see 等，使歌曲節奏分明、歌詞文體整齊，演唱起來朗朗上口，非常押韻。

The Beatles

Yesterday
寧回昨日

 英文歌詞

Yesterday all my troubles seemed so far away
Now it looks as though they're here to stay
Oh, I believe in yesterday

Suddenly, I'm not half the man I used to be
There's a shadow hanging over me
Oh, yesterday came suddenly

Why she had to go, I don't know, she wouldn't say
I said something wrong, now I **long for** yesterday

Yesterday love was such an easy game to play
Now I need a place to **hide away**
Oh, I believe in yesterday

Why she had to go, I don't know, she wouldn't say
I said something wrong, now I long for yesterday

Yesterday love was such an easy game to play
Now I need a place to hide away
Oh, I believe in yesterday

Ⅱ **詞彙註釋**

long for 渴望

hide away 躲藏

在《滾石》雜誌評選的「500 首有史以來最偉大的歌曲」中，這歌名列 13，在「100 首自 1963 年以來最偉大的英文歌曲」中高踞榜首。據《健力士世界紀錄大全》記載，它是有史以來翻唱次數最多的歌曲。

 中文譯文

昨日，我無慮無憂
今日，我無盡煩憂
噢，我寧回昨日

突然，我已徹頭徹尾改變
我的晴天一片陰暗
噢，昨日場景再次浮現

她不辭而別，離我而去
我寧回昨日，不再失言惹她生氣

昨日，愛情甜蜜而輕易
現在，我只想逃避
噢，我寧回昨日

她不辭而別，離我而去
我寧回昨日，不再失言惹她生氣

昨日，愛情甜蜜而輕易
現在，我只想逃避
噢，我寧回昨日

（李娟 譯）

 精彩之處

Shadow：本意為「陰影」，即「我被陰影籠罩」。翻譯中採取了意譯方法，將其譯為「我的晴天一片陰暗」，通過句內的強烈對比表現原意。

Oh, yesterday came suddenly：此處的 yesterday 不僅指時間上的昨天，更指發生在昨天的一切，屬於借代用法。翻譯中，將其借代意義翻譯出來，譯為「昨日場景再次浮現」。

Now I need a place to hide away：字面意思為「現在，我需要一個躲避的地方」，即「現在，我只想逃避」。對女友深沉的愛、女友的不辭而別讓男主人翁痛得不敢面對現實。這一句通過男主人翁的行為映射其無法忍受的內心之痛。

▶ NOW PLAYING

How Can You Mend a Broken Heart
心 傷 難 醫

 英文
歌詞

I can think of younger days when living for my life
Was everything a man could want to do
I could never see tomorrow
But I was never told about the sorrow

And how can you mend a broken heart
How can you stop the rain from falling down
How can you stop the sun from shining
What makes the world go round
How can you mend this broken man
How can a loser ever win
Please help me mend my broken heart
And let me live again

I can still feel the **breeze** that **rustles** through
the trees
And misty memories of days gone by
We could never see tomorrow
No one said a word about the sorrow

 詞彙
註釋

breeze *n.* 微風

rustle *v.* 發出沙沙聲

這首歌在 70 年代初奪下排行榜冠軍。如今專輯在全球累積銷售量已突破 1 億張大關的比吉斯樂隊（Bee Gees），是唯一在 20 世紀 60 年代到 90 年代都能奪得排行榜冠軍的歌手。擁抱過 7 次格林美獎的比吉斯樂隊，光榮地成為創作名人堂與搖滾名人堂一員，並獲全英音樂獎頒授「傑出貢獻獎」。

中文譯文

我想起了年輕時光
那時只想為自己而活
我看不見明日如何
可我並不知道悲傷

怎樣修補我受傷的心
怎樣阻止大雨落下
怎樣不讓太陽閃耀
是甚麼力量讓地球轉動
怎樣修補我受傷的心
失敗者怎樣才能勝利
幫幫我，修補我的受傷的心
讓我重獲新生

我感受到樹林裏
吹來的微風
模糊的記憶已經褪色
我再看不見明天
可是沒有人跟我提起過悲傷

精彩之處

mend my broken heart：這裏採用通感的修辭手法，使得心臟像其他東西一樣也能修補。

And misty...by：gone by 意為「消逝」，這裏省略了動詞 have。

（趙文譯）

Bee Gees
▶ N O W P L A Y I N G

How Deep Is Your Love
愛有多深

英文
歌詞

I know your eyes in the morning sun
I feel you touch me in the pouring rain
And the moment that you **wander** far from me
I wanna feel you in my arms again
And you come to me on a summer breeze
Keep me warm in your love and then softly leave
And it's me you need to show
How deep is your love

How deep is your love
How deep is your love
I really need to learn
'Cause we're living in a world of fools
Breaking us down
When they all should let us be
We belong to you and me

I believe in you
You know the door to my very soul
You're the light in my deepest darkest hour
You're my **savior** when I fall
And you may not think that
I care for you
When you know down inside
That I really do
And it's me, you need to show
How deep is your love

⏸ 詞彙
　註釋

wander *v.* 徘徊

savior *n.* 救世主

比吉斯樂隊（Bee Gees）由 3 個骨肉相連的親兄弟於英國曼徹斯特組成。這歌作為電影《週末狂熱》（*Saturday Night Fever*）的主題曲之一，其電影原聲帶成為 20 世紀 70 年代最受歡迎的專輯，帶動了當時的整個的士高風潮，並開出 4000 萬張的銷售狂潮，同時也開創了日後以歌曲為導向的電影原聲模式。

 中文譯文

晨輝中，我讀懂了你的眼神
傾盆大雨中我感覺到你的觸摸
你離我遠去時
我想把你再擁入懷中
夏日的微風中你來到我身邊
用你的愛溫暖我 然後悄然離去
你應該告訴我
你的愛有多深

你的愛有多深
你的愛有多深
我真的想知道
因為我們生活在愚人的世界
把我們打倒
那些愚人都這樣想
我們屬於彼此

我相信你
你知道通往我靈魂深處的門
你是我黑暗中的光明
你是我倒下時的救世主
也許你沒有意識到
我有多喜歡你
如果你讀懂我心
我是真的喜歡你
你應告訴我
你的愛有多深

（趙文 譯）

 精彩之處

I know...sun：「晨輝中，我讀懂了你的眼神」，體現了音樂中的柔情與審美。

pouring rain：指「傾盆大雨」。

wanna：該詞經常出現在詩歌和歌曲中，是 want to 的意思，這樣縮寫一方面是為了措辭簡潔，另外也是為了押韻的審美需要。

Bob Dylan
▶ N O W   P L A Y I N G

Blowing in the Wind
在風中飄蕩

How many roads must a man walk down
Before they call him a man
How many seas must a white dove sail
Before she sleeps in the sand
Yes, how many times must the cannon balls fly
Before they're forever banned
The answer, my friend, is blowing in the wind
The answer is blowing in the wind

Yes, how many years must a mountain exist
Before it is washed to the sea
Yes, how many years can some people exist
Before they're allowed to be free
Yes, how many times can a man turn his head
And pretend that he just doesn't see
The answer, my friend, is blowing in the wind
The answer is blowing in the wind

Yes, how many times must a man look up
Before he can see the sky
Yes, how many ears must one man have
Before he can hear people cry
How many deaths will it take
'Till he knows that too many people have died
The answer, my friend, is blowing in the wind
The answer is blowing in the wind

如果說貓王從形式上解放了搖滾樂，那麼卜戴倫（Bob Dylan）則從思想上解放了搖滾樂，真正賦予搖滾樂以靈魂。六七十年代美國社會出現了各種運動——民權運動、嬉皮士、反戰運動等。以此為題材的電影《阿甘正傳》（Forrest Gump），劇中有一幕感人的場景是女主角實現自己的夢想，在一家俱樂部演唱，她手抱結他，唱的正是這首歌。卜戴倫於2016年破格地以唱作人身份獲諾貝爾文學獎，成為佳話。

 中文譯文

一個人要走過多少條路
才能被真正稱之為人
一隻白鴿要飛越多少海洋
才能在沙灘上入眠
炮彈還要再飛行多少次
才會被永遠禁縛
我的朋友，答案在風中飄蕩
答案在風中飄蕩

一座山要屹立多少年
才會被沖蝕入海
一些人還要等待多少年
才能獲得自由
一個人能有多少次轉過頭去
佯裝甚麼都沒看見
我的朋友，答案在風中飄蕩
答案在風中飄蕩

一個人要仰望多少次
才能望見蒼天
一個人要有多少只耳朵
才能聽見人們的哭喊
還要犧牲多少生命
他才能明白已有太多人死去
我的朋友，答案在風中飄蕩
答案在風中飄蕩

（李音 譯）

 精彩之處

white dove： 象徵着和平，該句表達了人們渴望和平的願望。

cannon balls fly： 意為「炮彈紛飛」，這句歌詞道出了人們反戰的強烈要求。

mountain： 可理解為「種族歧視的大山」，歌詞表達人們反對種族歧視的強烈願望。

Don't You Think It's Time
難 道 你 不 覺 得

Don't you think it's time
Time to start a new
Time for changing views
Time for making up your mind

Don't you think it's time
Time for moving on
Time for growing strong
Time to leave the past behind

Don't you think it's time
Time for **quelling** fear
Time for a new year
Time for meaning what you say

Don't you think it's time
Time for **easing** doubt
Time for reaching out
Time to open up your eyes

Don't you think it's time
Time for trusting more
Without keeping score
Time to let forgiveness out

Don't you think it's time
Time for showing **grace**
Time for having faith
Time to make more of this time

You've been on my mind
Oh you've been on my mind

詞彙
註釋

quell *v.* 平息

ease *v.* 減輕

grace *n.* 優雅

卜伊雲斯（Bob Evans）是澳洲著名歌手。這首歌的歌詞充滿勵志色彩，引發聽眾對生活和未來的思考。以甚麼樣的姿態面對生活，決定着我們每個人不同的命運。

你不覺得現在是
重新開始的時刻
改變觀念的時刻
堅定決心的時刻

你不覺得現在是
繼續前進的時刻
厚積薄發的時刻
拋開過去的時刻

你不覺得現在是
戰勝恐懼的時刻
新一年開始時刻
說話算話的時刻

你不覺得現在是
緩解疑慮的時刻
張開懷抱的時刻
開闊視野的時刻

你不覺得現在是
加倍信任的時刻
不只看最終結果
寬恕原諒的時刻

秀秀儒雅的時刻
堅守信念的時刻
你不覺得現在是
發奮耕耘的時刻

你一直在我心裏
你一直在我心上

**精彩
之處**

keep score：是體育常用短語，表示比賽中的記分或得分，此處引申為關注最後成敗。

歌 中 new 和 view，on 和 strong，fear 和 year，doubt 和 out，more 和 score，grace 和 faith 等，兩兩押韻，發音飽滿響亮，和諧動聽。

（李穎　譯）

It's My Life
這 是 我 人 生

 英文歌詞

This ain't a song for the broken-hearted
No silent prayer for the faith-departed
I ain't gonna be just a face in the crowd
You're gonna hear my voice
When I shout it out loud

It's my life
It's now or never
I ain't gonna live forever
I just want to live while I'm alive
(It's my life)
My heart is like an open highway
Like **Frankie** said
I did it my way
I just wanna live while I'm alive
It's my life

This is for the ones who stood their ground
For Tommy and Gina who never backed down
Tomorrow's getting harder make no mistake
Luck ain't even lucky
Got to make your own breaks

⏸ **詞彙 註釋**

Frankie *n.* 弗蘭克 (這裏指 Frank Sinatra，弗蘭克·辛納屈，20 世紀流行音樂歌手，可與貓王和披頭四媲美，被稱為白人爵士歌王)

It's my life
It's now or never

Better stand tall when they're calling you out
Don't bend, don't break, baby, don't back down

邦·喬維（Bon Jovi）是當代美國的一支流行搖滾樂隊，擅長主流硬搖滾、金屬搖滾。此曲是專輯《迷戀》（*Crush*）中第一首單曲，2000 年 5 月 23 日發佈後，榮獲 ASCAP 流行音樂獎年度最佳歌曲之一。

 中文譯文

這首歌不是為心碎者而唱
也不是為失去信仰者默禱
我不甘願平凡一生
你定會聽到我的聲音
我會大聲吶喊

這是我人生
把握現在，機不再來
我不奢求永生
唯願把握有生之年
（這是我人生）
我的心像開放的高速公路
如弗蘭克所唱
我行我路
唯願把握有生之年
這是我人生

這首歌為堅守信念者而唱
為永不退縮的勞動者而唱
明日無疑更加艱辛
幸運女神不再眷顧
需要自己努力突破

這是我人生
把握現在，機不再來

遇到麻煩時挺直身子
不要屈服，不要放棄，不要退縮

（黃靈燕　譯）

 精彩之處

My heart...highway：把心比作高速公路，有開闊平坦之意。同時與後面說 I did it my way（我行我路）相互照應，其實也是說按自己的想法生活，好好把握現在。

it's now or never：把握現在，否則就永遠失去機會，暗示人生的短暫，因此我們要把握人生。

Don't bend, don't break, baby, don't back down：歌手在演唱這句時運用了略讀技巧。歌詞中 don't 的 [t], bend 中 [d], break 和 back 中末尾輔音 [k] 都省略不讀。另外，句中三個並列短句層層遞進，語氣強烈，表達了主人翁堅定的信心及不畏困難的勇氣。

No Matter What
無論如何

 No matter what they tell us
No matter what they do
No matter what they teach us
What we believe it's true

No matter what they call us
However they attack
No matter where they take us
We'll find our own way back

I can't deny what I believe
I can't be what I'm not
I know our love forever
I know no matter what

If only tears were laughter
If only night was day
If only prayers were answered
(Hear my prayers)
Then we could hear God say

And I will keep you safe and strong
And shelter from the storm
No matter where it's **barren**
A dream is being born

No matter who they follow
No matter where they leave
No matter how they judge us
I'll be everyone you need

No matter if the sun don't shine
(The sun don't shine)
Or if the skies are blue
(Skies are blue)
No matter what the end is
My life began with you

I can't deny what I believe
(What I believe)
I can't be what I'm not
I know this love's forever
That's all that matters now

**詞彙
註釋**

barren *adj.* 荒蕪的

1998 年，男孩地帶（Boyzone）的新歌加精選專輯《應邀》（*By Request*）發行，而先於專輯發行的這首單曲，作為愛情電影《摘星奇緣》（*Notting Hill*）主題曲大獲成功，擊敗《鐵達尼號》（*Titanic*）主題曲《我心永恆》（*My Heart Will Go On*）獲得英國全年總冠軍。男孩地帶擁有 4 張英國榜冠軍專輯，6 首冠軍單曲，唱片總銷量超過 2000 萬張。

 中文譯文

無論他們告訴我們甚麼
無論他們對我們做甚麼
無論他們教給我們甚麼
我們所堅信的才是真理

無論他們如何稱呼我們
無論他們如何譭謗我們
無論他們把我們帶到哪裏
我們終將找到回家的路

我無法忘記自己的信仰
我無法背叛自己的本性
我知道我們的愛將永恆
無論如何我都知道

多希望淚水能化為歡歌
多希望黑夜能變為白晝
多希望祈禱能得到回應
（傾聽我的祈禱）
我們就能聽到上帝之聲

我願保佑你安全與堅強
我願意為你去遮擋風雨
無論你的處境如何荒涼
一個新的夢想正在誕生

無論他們在追隨着何人
無論他們將要去向何處
無論他們如何評價我們
我將永遠都和你在一起

無論太陽是否照耀依舊
（陽光並不明媚）
無論天空是否蔚藍如初
（天空依舊蔚藍）
無論最終的結局如何
我的生命都因你而存在

我無法忘記自己的信仰
（我所信仰的）
我無法背叛自己的本性
我知道這份愛將會永恆
那才是現在最為重要的

（王孜　譯）

 精彩之處

no matter what：該短語出現多次，貫穿整首歌曲，與下文構成排比句式，並且作為歌曲題目，與全篇相互呼應，非常有音韻美。

If only...laughter：此處是虛擬語氣，表示作者的主觀意願，希望淚水能化為歡歌。此句與後兩句形成排比句式，且後兩句句法與該句相同。

$\mathscr{B}$ryan $\mathscr{A}$dams

▶ N O W   P L A Y I N G

(Everything I Do) I Do It for You
我 所 做 的 一 切

Look into my eyes, you will see
What you mean to me
Search your heart, search your soul
And when you find me there you'll search no more

Don't tell me it's not worth tryin' for
You can't tell me it's not worth dyin' for
You know it's true
Everything I do, I do it for you

Look into my heart, you will find
There's nothin' there to hide
Take me as I am, take my life
I would give it all, I would **sacrifice**

Don't tell me it's not worth dyin' for
I can't help it, there's nothin' I want more
You know it's true
Everything I do, I do it for you

There's no love, like your love
And no other, could give more love
There's nowhere, unless you're there
All the time, all the way

Oh, you can't tell me it's not worth tryin' for
I can't help it, there's nothin' I want more
I would fight for you, I'd lie for you
Walk the wire for you, ya I'd die for you
Ya know it's true
Everything I do, I do it for you

**詞彙
註釋**

sacrifice *v.* 犧牲

walk the wire 鋌而走
險

白賴仁·亞當斯（Bryan Adams）的作品多次入圍十大流行歌曲排行榜。這歌作為 1991 年電影《羅賓漢》（*Robin Hood: Prince of Thieves*）主題曲，甫推出就使亞當斯成為一位國際巨星。這首輕柔搖滾歌曲推出後，第一週就奪得美國和加拿大排行榜冠軍寶座，15 週內就創造了 300 萬張巨額銷量的神話，打破了 JA&M 公司的銷售紀錄，成為美國歷史上排名第二的單曲。

中文譯文

凝視我的雙眸，你會發現
你之於我如此重要
探尋你的心靈
直到發現我已在心底

不要說這不值得努力
不要說這不值得期待
你知道這是真實的
我做的一切，都是為你

看看我的心，你會發現
我無所隱藏
請接受真實的我，接受我真實的生活
我願給你一切，我願犧牲一切

不要說這不值得期待
我已深陷其中，我只要你
你知道這是真實的
我做的一切，都是為你

沒有一種愛像你的愛一樣
沒有人能愛我如此之深
你所在之地就是我的世界
無論何時何地

不要說這不值得努力
我已深陷其中，我只要你
我願為你奮鬥，我願為你撒謊
我願為你赴湯蹈火，我願為你而死
你知道這是真實的
我做的一切，都是為你

（黃靈燕　趙文　譯）

精彩
之處

Look into... see：首句歌詞很有意境，聽者甚至可以想像出男女主角深情對望，眼中只有彼此的畫面。

Everything I do, I do it for you：運用重複的手法，加強語氣，強調「我」為愛情付出的一切。

take my life：不是「取走我生命」的意思，而是與 take me as I am 句式一致，意思是「接受我真實的生活」。

I would fight... for you：四個並列句式，語氣強烈，表達了對愛情的忠貞不渝，願為此付出一切。
這句歌詞中出現了 fight、lie、wire、die 一系列單詞，採用相同的韻腳 [ai]，重讀並語氣逐漸加強，一步步展現出愛情的最高境界，最終達到高潮 I would die for you。

Carole King

You've Got a Friend
你 有 一 個 朋 友

英文
歌詞

When you're **down** and troubled
And you need some loving care
And nothing, nothing is going right
Close your eyes and think of me
And soon I will be there
To brighten up even your darkness night

You just call out my name
And you know wherever I am
I'll come running to see you again
Winter, spring, summer or fall
All you've got to do is call
And I'll be there
You've got a friend

If the sky above you
Grows dark and full of clouds
And that old north wind begins to blew
Keep your head together
And call my name out loud
Soon you'll hear me knocking at your door

You just call out my name
And you know whenever I am
I'll come running to see you again
Winter, spring, summer or fall
All you've got to do is call
And I'll be there Yes I will

Ain't it good to know that you've got a friend
When people can be so cold
They'll hurt you, and **desert** you
And take your soul if you let them
Oh, but don't you let them
You just call out my name

⏸ 詞彙
註釋

down *adj.* 情緒不高
的

keep one's head 鎮
靜

desert *v.* 放棄

這首歌收錄在卡洛兒·金（Carole King）個人第二張專輯《花毯》（Tapestry）中。這張專輯是史上最成功的專輯之一，它連續 15 週登上公告牌榜單的冠軍寶座，她也憑藉這張專輯獲得了四項格林美大獎，成就了她音樂事業上的第一個巔峰。這歌被很多歌手翻唱過，可謂經典中的經典。

中文譯文

當你情緒低落，心煩意亂時
當你需要愛與關懷時
當所有事情不如願時
閉上雙眼想着我
我就會在你身邊
照亮你漆黑的夜

只要你呼喊我的名字
無論我身在何處
都會立刻來到你身邊
無論春夏與秋冬
你只要一聲呼喊
我就會來到你身邊
你有一個朋友

若有一天你的天空
變暗，佈滿烏雲
寒冷的北風又吹起
保持鎮靜
大聲喊出我的名字
很快我就會出現在你門前

你只要一聲呼喊
無論我身在何處
都會立刻來到你身邊
無論春夏與秋冬
你只要一聲呼喊
我就會來到你身邊

知道有這樣一個朋友你會欣喜
人們可能會對你冷漠
傷害你，拋棄你
甚至連你的靈魂也帶走
但不要讓他們這般對你
大聲喊出我的名字

（葛婷婷　譯）

 精彩之處

go right：go 有「進行，運轉」之意，go right 本意是「正常運轉」，這裏表示「順利進行」。

I'll come running：這裏 running 作 come 的伴隨狀語，表示來的方式。running 一詞的使用生動形象地將主人翁急切想要趕過來的心情刻畫出來。

If the sky...clouds：將灰暗、佈滿烏雲的天空比喻成充滿艱難險阻的生活。

歌詞中生動地運用了押韻技巧，貫穿全曲，如 care 和 there，night 和 right，name 和 am，call 和 fall 等，豐富變換的韻腳使節奏感增強，發音富有層次感，鏗鏘有力，和諧動聽。

The Carpenters

Close to You
靠近你

英文
歌詞

Why do birds suddenly appear
Every time you are near
Just like me, they **long** to be
Close to you
Why do stars fall down from the sky
Every time you walk by
Just like me, they long to be
Close to you

On the day that you were born
The angels got together
And decided to create a dream come true
So they **sprinkled** moon dust in your hair of gold
And starlight in your eyes of blue

That is why all the girls in town
Follow you all around
Just like me, they long to be
Close to you

On the day that you were born
The angels got together
And decided to create a dream come true
So they sprinkled moon dust in your hair of gold
And starlight in your eyes of blue

詞彙
註釋

long *v.* 渴望

sprinkle *v.* 灑

That is why all the girls in town
Follow you all around
Just like me, they long to be
Close to you

卡朋特樂隊（The Carpenters）是一個聲樂與器樂的二人組合，由妹妹卡倫·卡朋特（Karen Carpenter）演唱，哥哥理查·卡朋特（Richard Carpenter）伴奏。在嘈雜、瘋狂的搖滾流行的 20 世紀 70 年代，以及人們面對社會的騷亂、家庭的代溝變得無助和絕望的時候，卡朋特兄妹以獨特的輕音樂風格成為最暢銷的音樂藝術家。

中文譯文

為甚麼鳥兒忽然出現
每當你走近的時候
像我一樣，它們都想
靠近你
為甚麼星星從天而降
每當你經過的時候
像我一樣，它們都想
靠近你

你出生那天
天使降臨
決定打造一個真實的夢境
於是在你的金髮上播撒月光
在你藍瞳裏點綴星光

這就是為甚麼鎮上所有的女孩兒
都圍着你打轉
就像我一樣，她們都渴望
靠近你

你出生那天
天使降臨
決定打造一個真實的夢境
於是在你的金髮上播撒月光
在你藍瞳裏點綴星光

這就是為甚麼鎮上所有的女孩兒
都圍着你打轉
就像我一樣，她們都渴望
靠近你

（胡微 譯）

精彩之處

Why do...appear/Why do ...sky：歌曲以兩個問句開始，配合着演唱者柔美的嗓音，似葉落，似水流，宛如午後外婆娓娓道來的故事，慢慢地鋪陳開來。

On the day...together：歌曲交代了為甚麼「你」如此的迷人，導致鎮上所有女孩都圍着「你」，原來是天使在「作怪」，這一切讓「你」看起來如此的不真實，讓我們如此渴望着要靠近「你」。

歌曲節奏明快，旋律優美。歌詞中也有很多尾韻的使用，如 appear 和 near，sky 和 by，true 和 blue，以及 town 和 around 等，豐富變換的尾韻使歌詞節奏感增強，發音更具層次感，體現音韻美與和諧美。

這首歌曾登上排行榜的冠軍寶座，並蟬聯了四個星期。樂隊獲得了該年度格林美「最佳新人」和「最佳流行合唱團體」兩項大獎。

The Carpenters

▶ N O W   P L A Y I N G

Yesterday Once More
昨 日 再 現

 英文歌詞

When I was young
I'd listen to the radio
Waiting for my favorite songs
When they played I'd sing along
It made me smile
Those were such happy times
And not so long ago
How I wondered where they'd gone
But they're back again
Just like a long lost friend
All the songs I love so well

Every sha-la-la-la
Every wo-wo still shines
Every shinga-linga-ling
That they're starting to sing so fine
When they get to the part
Where he's breaking her heart
It can really make me cry
Just like before
It's yesterday once more

Looking back on how it was
In years gone by
And the good time that I had
Makes today seem rather sad
So much has changed

It was songs of love
That I would sing to them
And I'd **memorize** each word
Those old **melodies**
Still sound so good to me
As they **melt** the years away

All my best memories
Come back clearly to me
Some can even make me cry
Just like before
It's yesterday once more

Ⅱ 詞彙
註釋

memorize *v.* 記住

melody *n.* 旋律

melt *v.* 融化

這首輕柔搖滾歌曲最早由理查·卡朋特（Richard Carpenter）和約翰·貝迪斯（John Bettis）創作於 1973 年，卡朋特樂隊（The Carpenters）將其收錄於專輯《此時，彼刻》（*Now & Then*）中並作為該專輯的主打歌曲，成為永恆暢銷單曲之一。

中文譯文

當我還很小的時候
我就喜歡收聽電台
等着我最愛的歌曲
音樂聲響我也跟着吟唱
那總讓我開心一笑
那些快樂的時光
就發生在不久以前
我在好奇它們何去
卻發現它們重新歸來
就像久違的朋友
所有我以前喜愛的歌曲

每一聲沙—啦—啦
每一聲喔—喔依舊富有魅力
每一聲淅—哩—哩
如今依舊動聽
當歌曲唱到
他讓她傷了心
我真的會淚流滿面
就像以前一樣
這就是昨日再現

如今我回頭再看
這麼多年過去
我所擁有的美好回憶
讓如今顯得多麼哀傷
因為很多已經發生改變

那些愛情的歌曲
那些我跟着吟唱的歌曲
那些我記得的歌詞
那些古老的旋律
如今依舊動聽
把歲月融化成了點滴

所有我最美好的回憶
都清晰湧回我的腦海裏
有些甚至讓我哭泣
就像以前一樣
這就是昨日再現

精彩之處

Those old melodies... away：非常富有詩意的一句歌詞，詞作者說音樂旋律將歲月融化成點滴，聽眾似乎腦海裏就會浮現山泉流淌的形象，整個畫面特別安靜清新，不由得會引起聽眾的某些回憶。

All my best... to me：這句歌詞很好地體現了英語的一個特點：以物作為主語。

（王晶 譯）

The Cascades

The Rhythm of the Rain
細 雨 滴 答

 英文
歌詞

Listen to the **rhythm** of the falling rain
Telling me just what a fool I've been
I wish that it would go and
Let me cry **in vain** and let me be alone again

The only girl I care about has gone away
Looking for a **brand new** start
But little does she know that when she left that day
Along with her she took my heart

Rain please tell me now does that seem fair
For her to steal my heart away
When she don't care
I can't love another
When my heart's somewhere far away

Rain won't you tell her that I love her so
Please ask the sun to set her heart **aglow**
Rain in her heart and
Let the love we knew start to grow

**⏸ 詞彙
註釋**

rhythm *n.* 韻律

in vain 徒然地

brand new 全新的

aglow *adj.* 發紅的

這是 60 年代美國瀑布合唱團（The Cascades）的歌曲，曾作為《阿甘正傳》（*Forrest Gump*）的插曲進入人們的視線。據美國廣電媒體的播放記錄顯示它曾在有史以來 100 首最受喜愛的西方歌曲中排第 9 名。

 中文譯文

聽窗外細雨在滴答
嘲笑我是多麼傻
期待它呀快走開
讓我默默憂傷哭泣吧

親愛的她已離開
尋找嶄新的未來
可她絲毫不知道
我的心已隨她遠離

雨啊這真是不公
為何她滿不在乎
我卻仍在獨徘徊
心門已不再打開
她才是唯一真愛

雨啊快把消息帶
傾訴對她的深愛
雨露滋潤她心海
愛情之芽復又生

 精彩之處

Rain...，aglow：這一句中將雨滴和太陽都擬人化。作者想要雨滴去告訴心愛的女孩自己還愛着她，他還希望雨滴能夠請太陽幫忙來滋潤女孩的心田，讓女孩能夠擁有熾熱的激情，來澆灌他們曾經枯萎的愛情之芽。這兩句不僅使男孩對女孩的癡情躍然紙上，也使男孩天真爛漫的情懷呼之欲出。

這首歌節奏活潑、明快，歌曲的前奏猶如滴答的雨聲，迷蒙、跳躍。歌中 Looking for a brand new start 和 Along with her she took my heart 具有相同的尾韻，發音時 start 和 heart 這一組尾韻也具有相同的節奏，發音飽滿，乾脆利索，戛然而止，給聽眾留下深刻的印象。

（李穎 譯）

Father and Son
父 與 子

英文
歌詞

【Father】 It's not time to make a change
Just **relax take it easy**
You're still young that's your fault
There's so much you have to know
Find a girl, **settle down**
If you want, you can marry
Look at me I am old
But I'm happy

I was once like you are now
And I know that it's not easy
To be calm when you've found
Something going on
But take your time think a lot
While think of everything you've got
For you will still be here tomorrow
But your dreams may not

【Son】
How could I try to explain
When I do it turns away again
And it's always been the same
Same old story
From the moment I could talk
I was ordered to listen
Now there's a way, and I know
That I have to go away
I know, I have to go

⏸ 詞彙
註釋

relax *v.* 放鬆

take it easy 慢慢來

settle down 定居

這首歌是專輯《農夫的茶》（*Tea for the Tillerman*）中的一首作品，由英國民謠搖滾代表人物凱特·史提芬斯（Cat Stevens）演唱，其中濃濃的父子深情隨音樂氤氳散開，潛入心底，聽罷讓人感動落淚。該專輯為史提芬斯的第四張專輯，也是其最為經典的專輯，發行於 1970 年，至今仍膾炙人口。

【父親】
改變之時還未到來
放鬆下來，一切慢慢來
年少輕狂是你的錯
仍有風雨等你經過
覓個女孩，心定下來
若心意相投，可今生共白頭
我雖年老
卻少煩惱

我也走過你這年紀
知道一切並不容易
切記保持冷靜
無論風雨還是天晴
適時停下腳步
反思身後走過的路
因為明天依舊要向前邁步
但你的夢想卻落腳此處

【兒子】
我該如何解釋
我時常感覺事事不得志
我總是同樣的理由
你總是同樣的要求
從我學會說話
就要聽這聽那
我知道，現在眼前有路
我要離你而去
是的，離你而去

精彩之處

（李娟　譯）

And it's...story： 在此處重複使用，更有力地渲染了兒子此時的無奈心情。

Morning Has Broken
破 曉

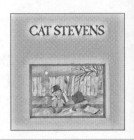

Morning has broken like the first morning
Blackbird has spoken like the first bird
Praise for the singing, praise for the morning
Praise for them springing fresh from the world

Sweet the rain's new fall, sunlit from heaven
Like the first **dewfall** on the first grass
Praise for the sweetness of the wet garden
Sprung in completeness where his feet pass

Mine is the sunlight; mine is the morning
Born of the one light Eden saw play
Praise with **elation**, praise every morning
God's **recreation** of the new day

Ⅱ 詞彙
註釋

blackbird *n.* 畫眉

dewfall *n.* 降露

spring *v.* 出現

elation *n.* 興高采烈

recreation *n.* 創造

凱特·史提芬斯（Cat Stevens）是英式民謠搖滾的代表人物，在世界各地唱片銷售量已超過 6000 萬張。1968 年凱特重返樂壇，創作新曲《破曉》（Morning Has Broken）並一舉奪得 1972 年成人抒情榜單曲冠軍。

中文譯文

天已破曉，如同第一個清晨開始
畫眉吟唱，如同第一隻鳥在歌唱
讚美歌唱，讚美清晨
讚美一切，為世界帶來新的生機

雨水初降，陽光閃耀，無限甜美
如同第一片新葉上的第一滴露珠
讚美雨後花園的清新
上帝在所到之處創造萬物

我是陽光，我是清晨
生於伊甸園的第一道光芒
欣然讚美，讚美每一個清晨
上帝都重創新的一天

精彩之處

這首歌改編自一首兒童讚美詩，讚美上帝帶來了黎明，每一天都是新的開始。作者為這首讚美詩輔上和旋，鋼琴與結他結合的伴奏，舒緩輕快。整首歌洋溢着細膩溫柔，單純美好，讓我們對黎明的到來充滿期待。

Born of...play：《創世紀》中：神看光是好的，就把光暗分開了。稱光為晝，暗為夜，有晚上，有早晨，這是第一日。因此，歌詞 the one light Eden saw play 指的是第一天。

（黃靈燕　譯）

Celine Dion
▶ N O W P L A Y I N G

My Heart Will Go On
我 心 永 恆

Every night in my dreams
I see you, I feel you
That is how I know you go on

Far across the distance
And spaces between us
You have come to show you go on

Near, far, wherever you are
I believe that the heart does go on
Once more you open the door
And you're here in my heart
And my heart will go on and on

Love can touch us one time
And last for a lifetime
And never let go till we're gone

Love was when I loved you
One true time I hold to
In my life we'll always go on

You're here, there's nothing I fear
And I know that my heart will go on
We'll stay forever this way
You are safe in my heart
And my heart will go on and on

這首歌為電影《鐵達尼號》（Titanic）的片尾曲，曾使席琳·迪翁（Celine Dion）在第 41 屆格林美頒獎儀式上獨拿兩項大獎，並獲得第 70 屆奧斯卡最佳電影歌曲。該曲在全球取得了名副其實的戰績，封頂各國單曲排行榜榜首，並成為全球最暢銷單曲之一，全球銷量過千萬。席琳也因這首主題曲而為全世界歌迷熟知，並一度創下每 3 秒鐘便賣出一張專輯的紀錄。

中文譯文

每晚的夢中
我都見到你，感覺到你
這就是我如何知道你會堅持不懈的

穿越距離
穿越時空
你到來向我訴說你會堅持不懈

無論遠近，無論天涯海角
我堅信我們的愛永無止境
再一次你打開了我的心扉
走進了我的內心
我心永恆

愛感動了你我
並將持續一生
直到我們死亡

愛就是我愛上你的那一刻
我真正想抓住的時候
我們的愛將永不止息

有你在，我無懼
我知道我心永恆
我們將永不分離
你在我心裏安然無恙
我心永恆

（壽業寧　譯）

精彩之處

That... go on： 我知道你將堅持不懈。go on 在此理解為對對方的愛將繼續。

And never... gone： 我們的愛永不會消失，直到我們死去。這句中 never...until，表達了彼此對愛情的忠貞不渝。

You're here... I fear： 你在此，我無懼，凸顯愛情的偉大力量，只要有對方在，就無所畏懼。

歌詞中反覆出現 go on，突顯了歌曲所要表達的愛情永無止境的主題，同時 go on 位於句尾，發音鏗鏘有力，語氣加強，聲音盤旋縈繞，有餘音繞樑之感，引起聽眾強烈的共鳴。

Paradise
天 堂

 英文歌詞

When she was just a girl
She expected the world
But it flew away from her reach
So she ran away in her sleep
And dreamed of para-para-paradise
Every time she closed her eyes

When she was just a girl
She expected the world
But it flew away from her reach
And the **bullets** catch in her teeth
Life goes on, it gets so heavy
The **wheel** breaks the butterfly
Every tear a waterfall
In the night, the **stormy** night
She closed her eyes
In the night, the stormy night
Away she flies

Dream of para-para-paradise
So lying underneath the stormy skies
She said, " I know the sun's set to rise
It's gonna be paradise"

🎵 詞彙
註釋

bullet *n.* 子彈

wheel *n.* 車輪

stormy *adj.* 暴風雨的

這是來自於英國著名流行樂隊酷玩樂隊（Coldplay）2011 年 9 月 12 日發行的一支單曲。單曲面世後廣受好評，並取得英國單曲榜第一的成績，成為英國歷史上登頂時間最長的單曲，也是該樂隊繼《生命萬歲》（*Viva La Vida*）之後的又一首登頂單曲。歌曲的 MV 贏得 2012 年度最佳搖滾視頻獎。

當她還是個女孩
她憧憬着這個世界
但那些美好都離她而去
因此她逃入夢中
想要夢到天堂
每次當她閉上雙眼

當她還是個女孩
她憧憬着這個世界
但那些美好都離她而去
子彈擊中目標
生活繼續着，但變得如此沉重
車輪碾碎了蝴蝶
每滴淚水都如泉湧
在暴風雨的夜晚
她閉上雙眼
在暴風雨的夜晚
她遠遠飛去

夢想着天堂
躺在暴風驟雨的天空之下
她説：「當太陽升起的時候
一定就是天堂」

（郭曉芹 譯）

 精彩之處

But it...： 這句話中的 it 指代前一句的 world，翻譯為「期待中美好的一切、夢想中的美好事物」；reach 不宜直譯，應翻譯為「期待中美好的一切都離她而去」。

The wheel...waterfall： 這兩句都用了隱喻的修辭手法，前面一句話用車輪碾過蝴蝶，比喻無情的現實摧殘着美麗而脆弱的靈魂；後面一句將眼淚比喻為瀑布一樣的水流，淋漓盡致地表現了女孩破碎的心靈。

Yellow
黃 色

Look at the stars, look how they **shine** for you
And everything you do
Yeah, they were all yellow
I came along, I wrote a song for you
And all the things you do
And it was called " yellow"

So then I took my turn
Oh what a thing to have done
And it was all **yellow**

Your skin, oh yeah your skin and bones
Turn into something beautiful
Do you know
You know I love you so

I swam across, I jumped across for you
Oh what a thing to do
'Cause you were all yellow
I drew a line, I drew a line for you
Oh what a thing to do
And it was all yellow

And your skin, oh yeah your skin and bones
Turn into something beautiful
Do you know
For you I bleed myself dry
It's true

**詞彙
註釋**

shine *v.* 閃爍

yellow *adj.* 膽小的

酷玩樂隊是英國搖滾樂壇進入新世紀之後崛起的最受歡迎的搖滾樂隊之一。該樂隊秉承了英式搖滾樂隊一貫的風格，成為英國新一代樂隊中的傑出代表。酷玩樂隊曾榮獲 2010 年 ASCAP 獎（美國作曲家、作家和出版商協會獎）年度創作人和年度單曲兩項大獎、2011 年英國 Q 音樂大獎最佳世界演出樂隊獎。

中文譯文

仰望空中繁星，看它們為你閃爍
你所做的一切
哦，它們都是黃色的
靠近你，我為你寫了首歌
你所做的一切
歌名是「黃色」

現在該到我了
哦，所做的每一件事
都是如此膽怯

你的肌膚，哦，你的肌膚和骨骼
是如此的美麗
你知道嗎
我是多麼愛你

我游向你，飛奔向你
該如何去做
讓你如此膽小
我勾勒出你的模樣
該如何去做
讓你如此膽小

你的肌膚，哦 你的肌膚和骨骼
變得如此美麗
你知道嗎
我願為你付出我的全部
這是真的

（壽業寧 譯）

精彩之處

酷玩樂隊因其第一支單曲《黃色》（Yellow）而成名，這支單曲曾衝上英國單曲榜的第 4 名。

And it was all yellow： yellow 一詞多次出現，有「黃色的」和「膽小的」兩層意思。在此表示膽小，缺乏勇氣。該詞充分表現了在喜歡的人面前那種既興奮而又膽小的心情。

draw a line： 指描繪線條，在此暗指作者的腦海中不斷出現對方，所以譯為「勾勒」更能形象地表現出對方在作者腦海中不斷浮現的畫面。

bleed dry： 意為「榨乾所有的錢」，在此理解為願意為對方付出一切。

The Cranberries

► N O W P L A Y I N G

Dreams
夢

 英文歌詞

Oh my life is changing everyday
In every possible way
And though my dreams
It's never quite as it seems
Never quite as it seems

I know I felt like this before
But now I'm feeling it even more
Because it came from you
Then I open up and see
The person **fumbling** here is me
A different way to be

I want more
Impossible to **ignore**
And they'll come true
Impossible not to do

And now I tell you openly
You have my heart so don't hurt me
For what I couldn't find
Talk to me amazing mind
So understanding and so kind
You're everything to me
'Cause you're a dream to me

 詞彙
註釋

fumble *v.* 摸索

ignore *v.* 忽視

這首另類搖滾歌曲出自於愛爾蘭卡百利樂隊（The Cranberries）的首張專輯，同時也是該專輯中最受歡迎的一首歌，這是該樂隊很有代表性的一首歌。歌曲節奏優美歡快，旋律明淨婉轉，主唱桃樂絲（Dolores）空靈的嗓音，細緻的吐氣，都使得這首歌溫暖美好，宛如天籟。王菲於 1994 年改編此曲成《夢中人》，並成為電影《重慶森林》的插曲，大受歡迎。

中文譯文

我的生活，每天都在改變
變化萬千
然而我的夢
卻從沒有實現
從沒有實現

我知道以前也是如此
然而此刻我的感受愈加強烈
因為它源自於你
我睜開雙眼，發現
困在原地的人是我
只不過是換了一種形式而已

我想要的更多
揮之不去
所有的夢想都會成真
一定可以

現在，我要當面告訴你
我已把心交給你
不要因為我的粗心而將我辜負
向我敞開你的心扉
你那麼溫柔，那麼體貼
你就是我的一切
因為你是我的夢

（楊爽　譯）

 **精彩
之處**

**It's never quite as it
seems:**「夢想沒有實現」。
作者開頭講「生活每天都
發生着變化」，然而夢想
依舊沒有實現，反映了她
的苦悶與無奈。

I know...before：在這個
句子中，有兩對對比，一
個是時間上的對比，before
與 now；另一個是情感上
的對比，通過 even more
二詞表現出來，已經從「感
覺到」轉變為「更深刻」。

這首歌之所以廣受歡迎，
其中一個重要原因是它具
有強烈的韻律美，尾韻
壓得特別好，如 day 和
way，dreams 和 seems，
以及 find、mind 和 kind。

The Cranberries

Zombie
麻木的人

Another head **hangs** lowly
Child is slowly taken
And the **violence** caused such silence
Who are we mistaken

But you see it's not me
It's not my family
In your head, in your head
They are fighting
With their tanks, and their bombs
And their bombs, and their guns
In your head
In your head they are crying

In your head, in your head
Zombie, zombie, zombie
What's in your head, in your head
Zombie, zombie, zombie

Another mother's breaking
Heart is taking over
When the violence causes silence
We must be mistaken

It's the same old theme since 1916
In your head
In your head they're still fighting
With their tanks, and their bombs
And their bombs, and their guns
In your head
In your head they are dying
In your head, in your head

詞彙
註釋

hang *v.* 低垂

violence *n.* 暴力

卡百利樂隊（The Cranberries）是來自愛爾蘭的四人團體，他們以愛爾蘭式的細膩抒情和惆悵旋律，唱出了崇尚和平，關懷世界的理念。這歌是他們經典的另類搖滾歌曲之一，曾獲得 1995 年全歐 MTV 音樂大獎「年度最佳歌曲」。

又一顆頭顱垂下
孩子的生命漸漸流失
暴力導致了這死寂
我們之中誰在犯罪

但你看不是我
也不是我的家人
在你的腦海中，在你的腦海中
他們在殘殺
用坦克，用炮彈
用炮彈，用槍支
在你的腦海中
在你的腦海中他們在哭泣

在你的腦海中，在你的腦海中
麻木的人，麻木的人，麻木的人
甚麼留在你的腦海中，你的腦海中
麻木的人，麻木的人，麻木的人

又一位心碎的母親
失去了靈魂
暴力導致了這死寂
我們都是罪人

這是 1916 年以來的永恆悲劇
在你的腦海中
在你的腦海中他們仍在殘殺
用坦克，用炮彈
他們的炮彈，他們的槍
在你的腦海中
他們在你的腦海中死去
在你的腦海中，在你的腦海中

（宋思怡　譯）

精彩之處

Another head...lowly：
這句話中 head 指的是孩子的頭。又一個孩子垂下了頭，即又一個孩子死去的意思，歌曲的第一句便營造了一種死寂的氛圍，表現出戰爭的殘酷。

zombie： 歌曲中不斷重複這個詞，是歌手對戰爭的控訴，是發自肺腑的吶喊。

Another mother's breaking： 這裏「心碎的母親」與前文中「死去的孩子」是兩個相互關聯的意象，共同為控訴戰爭，呼喚和平的主題服務。

The Cure
▶ N O W   P L A Y I N G

Friday I'm in Love
星 期 五 我 戀 愛 了

英文歌詞

I don't care if Monday's blue
Tuesday's grey and Wednesday too
Thursday I don't care about you
It's Friday I'm in love

Monday you can fall apart
Tuesday Wednesday break my heart
Oh Thursday doesn't even start
It's Friday I'm in love

Saturday wait
And Sunday always comes too late
But Friday never hesitate

I don't care if Monday's black
Tuesday Wednesday heart attack
Thursday never looking back
'Cause it's Friday I'm in love

Monday you can hold your head
Tuesday Wednesday stay in bed
Or Thursday watch the walls instead
It's Friday I'm in love

Dressed up to the eyes
It's a wonderful surprise
To see your shoes and your spirits rise
Throwing out your **frown**
And just smiling at the sound
And as **sleek** as a shriek
Spinning round and round
Always take a big bite
It's such a **gorgeous** sight
To see you eat in the middle of the night
You can never get enough
Enough of this stuff
It's Friday I'm in love

⏸ 詞彙
註釋

dress up 盛裝打扮

frown *n.* 蹙額

sleek *adj.* 光滑的

spin *v.* 旋轉

gorgeous *adj.* 華麗的

還記得《每天愛你第一次》（*50 First Dates*）那種怦然心動的感覺嗎？作為片中的插曲，這首另類搖滾歌曲將淒慘浪漫的失憶愛情故事演繹得更加生動感人。此曲曾在 1992 年奪得由觀眾投票選出的 MTV 最佳視頻音樂獎。治療樂隊（The Cure）治癒着聽眾們的心。

中文譯文

我不在乎星期一讓人憂鬱
星期二星期三的陰霾
星期四我不在乎你
星期五我戀愛了

星期一你可以選擇離開
星期二星期三讓我心碎
哦， 星期四甚至還未到來
星期五我戀愛了

星期六等待
星期天總是姍姍來遲
但是星期五從未遲到過

我不在乎星期一是否讓人絕望
星期二星期三讓人歇斯底里
星期四從不回首往事
因為星期五我戀愛了

星期一你可以昂首挺胸
星期二星期三臥床休息
或者星期四對着牆壁發呆
星期五我戀愛了

盛裝打扮，衣着光鮮
這是一個巨大的驚喜
看你鞋子精美，興致高漲
別再皺眉
聽着音樂微笑吧
尖叫着發洩着不爽
不停地轉着圈兒
總是搶佔着大部分人的視線
這是如此絢麗的景象
看着你在午夜饕食
你永遠也不滿足
對它們感到滿足
星期五我戀愛了

（胡微 譯）

精彩之處

英語中常用顏色來表示人的心情和情緒，歌詞中的 blue 就常指人們情緒低落，憂鬱；grey 則象徵着陰霾，表示人們心情很沉悶；black 反映出鬱悶等糟糕的負面情緒。

乍一聽這首歌會讓人覺得很滑稽——週一無所謂；週二週三沒約會；週四等待；週五等愛來——這般無厘頭的歌詞卻讓人覺得十分歡樂。看似是對整個星期的總結，但事實上卻是對整個愛情過程的總結。

這首歌詼諧幽默，歌詞更是將押韻技巧運用到了極致。 歌 中 blue 和 too，heart 和 start，wait 和 late、sound 和 round 等構成豐富的尾韻，發音和諧動聽，體現音韻美。

Daniel Powter

Best of Me
完 美 綻 放

I wasn't mean the wrong way
Won't you do me the right way
Where you gonna be tonight
'Cause I won't stay too long

Maybe you're the life for me
When you talk to me it strikes me
Won't somebody help me
'Cause I don't feel too strong

Was there something that I said
Was there something that I did
Or the **combination** of both that did me in

You know I'm hoping you sing alone
Even it's not your favorite song
Don't wanna be there
When there's nothing left to say
You know that some of us spin again
When you do you need a friend
Don't wanna be there
When there's nothing left for me
And I hate the thought finally been **erased**
Baby that's the best of me

Everything's behind you
But the hopeless signs beside you
Living in the moment
Have I wasted all your time

詞彙
註釋

combination *n.* 結合

erase *v.* 抹除

此曲自 2008 年發行後光環經久不退,演唱者正是曾經名噪歐美歌壇的加拿大吟唱詩人——丹尼爾·波特(Daniel Powter)。他真假音駕馭自如,每首歌都跌宕起伏而不單調。細膩獨特的感染力及出色的琴藝為其贏得了「城市琴人」的美譽。

我曾迷失了方向
期許你能為我引指道路
今夜你要去往何方
因為我不能逗留太久

也許你是我的生命
與你暢談,總有觸動
多想有人能幫我
我不願故作堅強

是我說了甚麼
或是做過甚麼
還是兩者都有,讓我陷入此境

我希望你能縱情高歌
即使歌非所愛
我不願如風般靜默
四目相視無言以對
記憶點滴,縈繞心間
這時你需要朋友陪伴
當你不需要我時
我會轉身離去
我痛恨終將被你遺忘
親愛的,那曾是最美的我

你拋卻一切
但絕望卻伴你左右
時至今日
我是否誤你年華太多

(趙瑋 譯)

I was...way:mean 為 打算,意欲如何的意思,因此 wasn't mean the wrong way 指曾經有過錯,但都是無心為之,即誤入歧途,與後半句中的 do me the right way 形成對應,一錯一改,突出曲中 you 對主角人生選擇的重要意義。

strike:不是「打擊」的意思。strike 帶有「打動,旁敲側擊」之意,且影響力相對持續,不比 influence 那般抽象和輕描淡寫,也不比 hit 或 beat 一般力度過重,因此作詞人巧妙地用這一詞形容對方言語與思想為主人翁帶來的心靈觸動、感化啟迪,尺度把握與表達效果都恰到好處。

spin:該詞釋義極為豐富,在不同語境下的意義大相徑庭,此處可理解為「閃現,圍繞」,形象呈現了對陳情舊事欲忘不能,甜蜜瞬間反覆重現的現實狀態。

Daniel Powter

Free Loop
管不住的音符

 英文歌詞

I'm a little used to calling outside your name
I won't see you tonight so I can keep from going
insane
But I don't know enough, I get some kinda lazy day

I've been **fabulous** through to fight my town a
name
I'll be **stooped** tomorrow if I don't leave as them
both the same
But I don't know enough, I get some kinda lazy day

'Cause it's hard for me to lose
In my life I've found only time will tell
And I will figure out that we can baby
We can do a **one night stand**, yeah

And it's hard for me to lose in my life
I've found outside your skin right near the fire
That we can baby
We can change and feel alright

I'm a little used to wandering outside the rain
You can leave me tomorrow if it suits you just the
same
But I don't know enough
I need someone who leaves the day

**⏸ 詞彙
註釋**

insane *adj.* 瘋狂的

fabulous *adj.* 神話似
的

stoop *v.* 侮辱

one night stand 一夜
夫妻

這首歌是加拿大「城市琴人」丹尼爾·波特（Daniel Powter）首張同名專輯中的第二首歌曲。丹尼爾有深厚的鋼琴功底，能夠自如地駕馭真假音。他的歌曲跌宕起伏，巧妙琢磨，歌詞也有很強的感染力，輕快活潑又不失古靈精怪。

中文譯文

我有些習慣喊你的名字
我今晚不會見你
否則我會發瘋
但我不太明白，為甚麼我的日子變得有些懶散

我曾經為我的小鎮贏得名聲
英勇地像個神話
如果我明天不像他們一樣離開
就會被凌辱欺壓
但我不太明白，為甚麼我的日子變得有些懶散

因為我一生很少失敗
我發現只有時間才能證明這一切
我堅信，親愛的
我們可以一夜盡歡

我一生很少失敗
你的皮膚熱情如火
因此我相信，親愛的
我們可以改變，可以過得很好

我有些習慣漫步在雨中
明天你可以離開我
如果這樣對你也好
但我不太明白這是怎麼了
我需要那天有人離開

（張旋 譯）

精彩之處

歌曲中混有玄妙的琴聲，假聲游離，帶給聽者一種慵懶的、歡快的感覺，彷彿一個詩人站在寂寞的湖畔，眼神高傲又倔強。

used to 常常與 be，get，become 等詞連用，後接名詞或動名詞表示習慣於。

both the same：此處是指「我」與「他們」一樣（離開）。same 與上句末的 name 押韻，使歌曲更加朗朗上口。

I've found outside...fire：此句用如火的皮膚比喻戀人表現出來的炙熱的感情和慾望。

Dido

▶ N O W   P L A Y I N G

Life for Rent
漂泊人生

 英文
歌詞

I haven't really ever found a place that I call home
I never stick around quite long enough to make it
I apologize that once again I'm not in love
But it's not as if I mind that your heart ain't exactly breaking
It's just a thought, only a thought

But if my life is for rent
And I don't learn to buy
Well I **deserve** nothing more than I get
'Cause nothing I have is truly mine

I've always thought that
I would love to live by the sea
To travel the world alone and live my life more simply
I have no idea what's happened to that dream
'Cause there's really nothing left here to stop me
It's just a thought, only a thought

But if my life is for rent and I don't learn to buy
While my heart is a **shield** and I won't let it down
While I am so afraid to fail so I won't even try
Well how can I say I'm alive

If my life is for rent
And I don't learn to buy
Well I deserve nothing more than I get
'Cause nothing I have is truly mine

⏸ 詞彙
註釋

deserve *v.* 應得

shield *n.* 盔甲

這首歌是英國創作才女蒂朵（Dido）的作品，收錄於其同名專輯中。蒂朵是英國樂壇史上最暢銷女歌手，兩張專輯全球銷售突破 2200 萬張，她也是 2004 世界音樂獎全英最暢銷歌手。這首歌慵懶纏綿，帶有淡淡的傷感，同時含有鞭策自己的意味。

 中文譯文

我從未找到一個可以稱為家的地方
因為我總是來去匆匆
再一次悔恨，可不得不又離開
我痛切感知
你的心一定在流淚
這只是個念想，一個念想

如果我一生漂泊
卻不懂如何安定
那我不值得擁有更多
因為我有的也不真正屬於我

以前我一直覺得
我喜歡傍海而居
獨自旅行
簡單生活
我不知道這個夢為甚麼沒有實現
因為事實上我已沒甚麼牽絆
這只是一個念想，一個念想

如果我一生漂泊卻不懂如何安定
若我心中有防備如盔甲，不願卸下
若我害怕失敗，不敢嘗試
那我怎麼能算真正活着

如果我一生漂泊
卻不懂如何安定
那我不值得擁有更多
因為我有的也不真正屬於我

（張旋 譯）

 精彩之處

I never stick around...it： 在一個地方待久了就產生一種「家」的歸屬感，但我從來沒有。形容詞 +enough to 是一種常見結構，意思是「足夠……去做」。make 在這裏是「使……成功」的意思，it 代指上句。

for rent： 意為「房屋出租」，這句話將人生比喻成房屋，也就是說「我」要一生漂泊。

nothing more than： 意為「不比……多，僅僅」。

Thank You
謝 謝

英文
歌詞

My tea's gone cold
I'm wondering why I got out of bed at all
The morning rain clouds up my window and I can't
see at all
And even if I could it'd all be grey
But your picture on my wall
It reminds me that it's not so bad
It's not so bad

I drank too much last night, got bills to pay
My head just feels in pain
I missed the bus and there'll be hell today
I'm late for work again
And even if I'm there
They'll all **imply** that I might not last the day
And then you call me and it's not so bad
It's not so bad and

I want to thank you for giving me the best day of
my life
Oh, just to be with you is having the best day of
my life

Push the door, I'm home at last and I'm **soaking**
through and through
Then you handed me a towel and all I see is you
And even if my house falls down now
I wouldn't have a clue
Because you're near me

⏸ 詞彙
註釋

imply *v.* 暗指

soak *v.* 浸泡

這首歌是英國創作歌手蒂朵（Dido）第一張專輯《沒有天使》（*No Angel*）中的成名作，為年度十大熱門歌曲之一。這首歌被電影《緣份兩面睇》（*Sliding Doors*）選為主題曲。專輯幾次進入英國榜，在超過 35 個國家被評為白金專輯，全球銷量達 2100 萬，是 21 世紀以來全英銷量第二多的專輯。

 中文譯文

杯子裏的茶涼了
我為甚麼要從床上爬起來
晨雨模糊了窗子
我甚麼也看不到
除了牆上你的照片
我滿目皆灰
它提醒着我情況沒那麼糟
沒那麼糟

昨晚喝得太多，還有帳單要付
頭太疼了
錯過了班車，今天將如煉獄般
又一次上班遲到
即使到班
他們也會暗暗認為我撐不過一天
而後，你的電話讓我感到情況沒那麼糟
沒那麼糟

想道聲謝謝
你給了我生命中最美好的一天
哦，和你在一起
就是我生命中最好的時光

推開門，終於到家了
像個落湯雞
你遞來毛巾，我陶醉在你的愛中
即使現在山崩地裂
我也無所感知
因為你在我身邊

（喬楠 譯）

 精彩之處

through and through：
意為「完全地」，這句就是全身都被雨水澆透的意思。

all I see is you： 歌中的主人翁當時處於熱戀的狀態，所以眼中只有心中所愛之人，其實就是「陶醉在你的愛中」之意。

my house falls down now： 戀愛的美好感覺可以讓人不顧一切，所以翻譯成「山崩地裂」更符合漢語表達。

Don McLean

▶ N O W P L A Y I N G

American Pie
美國派

英文
歌詞

A long long time ago
I can still remember how that music used to make me smile
And I knew if I had my chance
That I could make those people dance
And maybe they'd be happy for a while.
But February made me shiver
With every paper I'd deliver
Bad news on the doorstep
I couldn't take one more step
I can't remember if I cried
When I read about his **widowed** bride
But something touched me deep inside
The day the music died

So Bye-bye, Miss American Pie
Drove my chevy to the **levee**
But the levee was dry
And them good old boys were drinkin' whiskey and rye
Singin' this'll be the day that I die

Did you write the Book of Love
And do you have faith in God above
If the Bible tells you so
Now do you believe in rock 'n roll
Can music save your **mortal** soul
And can you teach me how to dance real slow

Well, I know that you're in love with him
'Cause I saw you dancin' in the gym
You both kicked off your shoes
Man, I dig those rhythm and blues

I was a lonely teenage broncin' buck
With a pink **carnation** and a pickup truck
But I knew I was out of luck
The day the music died

**⏸ 詞彙
註釋**

widowed *adj.* 寡居的

levee *n.* 碼頭

mortal *adj.* 凡人的

carnation *n.* 康乃馨

這是一首用音樂記錄美國六十年代歷史的史詩性歌曲。這首歌曾登上英國排行榜第二、美國排行榜第一，其同名專輯也大獲成功。

很久很久以前
我依然記得 那時音樂總能使我微笑
我知道 如果我有機會
我能使那些人翩翩起舞
也許他們能快樂好一陣子
但是二月使我不寒而慄
因為我遞出的每一份報紙
都將噩耗帶到門前
我無法向前一步
我不記得自己有沒有哭
當讀到他那位遺孀的消息時
但有一種東西深深觸動了我
那天，音樂死了

那麼，再見了，美國派小姐
開着我的雪佛蘭到了碼頭
但是碼頭已經乾涸
那些老男孩們喝着黑麥威士忌
唱着「這將是我死的那一天」

是你寫的愛之書嗎
你會相信上帝嗎
如果聖經這麼告訴你
你相信搖滾嗎
音樂可以拯救你的靈魂嗎
你可以教我如何慢舞嗎

我知道你愛上了他
因為我看到你們在體育館裏起舞
舞到你們雙雙踢掉了鞋子
天啊，我深深感受到了節奏藍調

那時的我是個寂寞的年輕人
拿着粉色康乃馨，駕着皮卡車
但我知道自己不走運
那天，音樂死了

精彩之處

But February made me shiver： 1959 年 2 月，早期搖滾的代表人物 Buddy Holly 及另兩位搖滾巨星所搭乘的航班墜毀，三人均遇難，這個消息對於 Dan Mclean 來說非常震驚，所以二月使他不寒而慄。

broncin' buck： broncin' 即 broncing（美國口語），= bronco「野馬」；buck 是「小夥子」的意思。

（張玉嬌 譯）

Don McLean

Vincent
文 森 特

英文
歌詞

Starry, starry night
Paint your **palette** blue and gray
look out on a summer's day
With eyes that know the darkness in my soul
Shadows on the hills
Sketch the trees and the daffodils
Catch the breeze and the winter chills
In colors on the snowy linen land

Now I understand
What you tried to say to me
How you suffered for your **sanity**
How you tried to set them free
They would not listen
They did not know how
Perhaps they'll listen now

Starry, starry night
Flaming flowers that brightly blaze
Swirling clouds in violet haze
Reflect in Vincent's eyes of China blue
Colors changing hue
Morning fields of amber grain
Weathered faces lined in pain
Are soothed beneath the artist's Loving hand

For they could not love you
But still your love was true
And when no hope was left inside
On that starry, starry night
You took your life
As lovers often do
But I could have told you, Vincent
This world was never meant for one
As beautiful as you

Starry ,starry night
Portaits hang in empty halls
Frameless heads on hameless walls
With eyes that watch the world and can't forget

Like the stranger that you've met
The ragged men in ragged clothes
The silver thorn of bloddy rose
Live crushed and broker on the virgin snow

⏸ 詞彙
註釋

palette *n.* 調色板

sketch *v.* 素描

sanity *n.* 清醒

這首歌是著名民謠歌手唐·麥克萊恩（Don McLean）為了悼念荷蘭畫家梵高（Vincent van Gogh）而創作的。麥克萊恩用這首充滿憂傷的歌獻給「瘋子」梵高，在感動自己的同時，也感動了全世界熱愛生活的人們。

中文譯文

繁星閃耀的夜晚
在調色板抹上灰與藍
夏日裏的輕輕一瞥
便將我靈魂的陰暗洞穿
群山的陰影
描繪出樹木與水仙的輪廓
用雪地斑駁的色彩
捕捉着風的呼吸與冬的凜冽

如今我才讀懂
你想要訴說的心聲
你如何因清醒備受煎熬
你多希望思想掙脫束縛
他們不加理會
也不懂得傾聽
也許他們永遠不會聽

繁星閃耀的夜晚
絢爛的花朵盛放如烈焰
繾綣的雲朵染上紫色暮靄
映在文森特湛藍的眼中
色彩流轉
清晨琥珀色的麥田
飽經風霜與苦痛的臉孔
在畫家充滿愛意的筆下得到撫慰

只因他們並不愛你
你的愛卻真摯如初
當希望隕落
在那繁星閃耀的夜晚
你結束了生命
如愛人殉情一般
文森特，我本該告訴你
這個世界本就配不上
你這般美麗的生靈

繁星閃耀的夜晚
空蕩的大廳掛着畫像
無框的頭像倚靠在無名的牆上
那些注視着世間卻無法忘懷的世界

就像曾相遇過的陌生人
可憐的人穿着破爛的衣服
就像血紅玫瑰上的銀刺
飽受踐踏後扔在潔白的雪地上

（宋思怡 譯）

精彩之處

starry night： 指的是梵高的畫作《星夜》。歌曲中還包含着梵高的其他畫作，如 weathered faces lined in pain 指的是《自畫像》；flaming flowers that brightly blaze 描寫的是畫作《向日葵》。

Hotel California
加州旅館

On a dark desert highway, cool wind in my hair
Warm smell of colitas, rising up through the air
Up ahead in the distance, I saw a **shimmering** light
My head grew heavy and my sight grew dim
I had to stop for the night
There she stood in the doorway
I heard the mission bell
And I was thinking to myself
This could be heaven or this could be hell
Then she lit up a candle and she showed me the way
There were voices down the corridor
I thought I heard them say

Welcome to the Hotel California
Such a lovely place
Such a lovely face
Plenty of room at the Hotel California
Any time of year, you can find it here

Her mind is Tiffany twisted, she got the Mercedes bends
She got a lot of pretty, pretty boys, that she calls friends
How they dance in the courtyard, sweet summer sweat
Some dance to remember, some dance to forget

So I called up the captain,
"Please bring me my wine"
He said, "we haven't had that spirit here since 1969"
And still those voices are calling from far away

這首歌出自老鷹樂隊（Eagles）的歌曲同名專輯，是一首非常經典的結他歌曲。1977 年 5 月，此曲位於最熱 100 首單曲排行榜榜首，當年連續八週獲得排行榜冠軍。樂隊不僅是格林美大獎的常客，每張唱片都是金唱片的驕子。

我走在漆黑荒蕪的高速路上，寒風吹起我的頭髮
溫馨的大麻香在空中彌漫
就在前面不遠的地方，我看見了一束閃爍的燈光
腦袋已經疲乏，眼神已經暗淡
我需要找個地方度過這漆黑的夜晚
這時我看見站在門口的她
遠處傳來教堂大鐘的聲響
於是我暗自思忖
這也許是天堂，亦可能是煉獄
她將蠟燭點燃，為我指明了方向
走廊下面有人在說話
我似乎聽見他們說

歡迎來到加州旅館
多麼溫馨的地方
多麼可愛的臉龐
這裏有無數的客房
無論何時你都能找到這個地方

她的腦海裏盡是珠寶，她坐上的車是那麼豪華
她的身邊圍繞着漂亮的男孩，可是她卻喊他們玩伴
他們在園中盡情歡跳，把甘甜的汗珠盡情揮灑
有人跳舞為了銘記，有人卻是為了遺忘

我喊來旅館領班：
「請為我端上葡萄酒」
他說：「1969 年後就不再供應」
遙遠的地方又傳來說話聲

Wake you up in the middle of the night
They livin' it up at the Hotel California
ust to hear them say…
Welcome to the Hotel California
Such a lovely place (Such a lovely place)
Such a lovely face
They livin' it up at the Hotel California
What a nice surprise (what a nice surprise)
Bring your alibis

Mirrors on the ceiling
The pink champagne on ice
And she said "We are all just prisoners here, of
our own device"
And in the master's chambers
They gathered for the feast
They stab it with their steely knives
But they just can't kill the beast

Last thing I remember, I was
Running for the door
I had to find the passage back
To the place I was before
"Relax, " said the night man
"We are programmed to receive.
You can check-out any time you like,
But you can never leave! "

II 詞彙
註釋

shimmering *adj.* 閃
爍的

在夜半將你鬧醒
他們在加州旅館盡情狂歡
我聽見他們說
歡迎來到加州旅館
如此美好的樂園
如此美麗的面容
他們在這兒狂歡
多麼美妙的驚喜
是你有來這兒的藉口

盯着天花板上的鏡子
我喝着冰涼香檳
而她說：
「我們都是自願來這的囚犯」
在主子的房間
大家聚集赴宴
他們用小刀刺向獵物
但沒有人能殺死那可怕的怪獸

我所記得的最後一件事
是我朝着門口奔去
但怎麼也找不到路
回不到我進來的地方
「放輕鬆點」守夜人突然對我說：
「我們照常接待旅客
你隨時可以結帳
但你永遠逃不出這裏」

（王晶 譯）

 **精彩
之處**

colitas：西班牙語詞，意
思為「小尾巴」。70 年代，
大麻的苞蕾被戲稱為小尾
巴，因此這裏的 colitas 指
的是大麻。

Her mind... bend：
Tiffany 是珠寶的代名詞，
Mercedes bends（梅賽
德斯 - 賓士）是豪華車的
代名詞，但是賓士的標
牌是 Benz，這裏卻用了
bends，是為了與前文的
twist 呼應，表示女孩內心
已經被奢華的物質享受所
扭曲。

Eddie Vedder

No Ceiling
無疆

Comes the morning
When I can feel
That there's nothing left to be **concealed**
Moving on a scene **surreal**
No, my heart will never, will never be far from here

Sure as I am breathing
Sure as I'm sad
I'll keep this wisdom in my **flesh**
I leave here believing more than I had
And there's a reason I'll be, a reason I'll be back

As I walk the **hemisphere**
I got my wish to up and disappear
I've been wounded, I've been healed
Now for landing I've been
For landing I've been cleared

Sure as I am breathing
Sure as I'm sad
I'll keep this wisdom in my flesh
I leave here believing more than I had
This love has got no ceiling

 詞彙
註釋

conceal *v.* 隱藏

surreal *adj.* 超現實的

flesh *n.* 肉體

hemisphere *n.* 半球

這首《荒野生存》（*Into the wild*）的電影插曲由艾迪·維達（Eddie Vedder）演唱，並收錄於電影同名專輯中。該專輯首次進榜就衝到公告牌專輯榜的第 11 位。整首歌簡潔流暢，簡單的結他彈唱傳達着對自然和野性的嚮往，也激勵着人們對自由和真理的尋找。

 中文譯文

黎明來到
我能感到
一覽無遺的純淨
走向如夢的仙境
我的心永遠不會，永遠不會遠離

如我一樣的呼吸
如我一樣的悲傷
這感悟必將存於我的骨血
我離開之時心中更加堅信
我終將回歸，終將回歸

我周遊世界
夢想起起落落
受傷，治癒
如今我終尋得歸宿
尋得歸宿

如我一樣的呼吸
如我一樣的悲傷
這感悟必將存於我的骨血
我離開之時心中更加堅信
此愛無疆

（宋思怡　譯）

 精彩之處

這首歌出現在電影《荒野生存》的結尾處，音樂響起時，男主角正在收拾行囊，準備離開。

Moving on a scene surreal：指的是走向夢一般的風景。

This love has got no ceiling：ceiling 是「極限」的意思，整句話是指這份愛沒有極限。這裏的 love 並非指愛情，而指的是男主角對自然的愛，這份愛已深入骨髓，與他的呼吸共存，永不消失。

Can You Feel the Love Tonight
今 夜 ， 你 可 感 受 到 我 的 愛

 英文 歌詞

There's a calm **surrender** to the rush of day
When the heat of the rolling wind can be turned away
An **enchanted** moment, and it sees me through
It's enough for this restless **warrior**
Just to be with you

And can you feel the love tonight
It is where we are
It's enough for this wide-eyed wanderer
That we got this far

And can you feel the love tonight
How it's laid to rest
It's enough to make kings and **vagabonds**
Believe the very best

There's a time for everyone if they only learn
That the twisting **kaleidoscope** moves us all in turn
There's a rhyme and reason to the wild outdoors
When the heart of this star-crossed voyager beats in time with yours

⏸ 詞彙 註釋

surrender to 屈 服 於，聽任

enchanted *adj.* 美妙 的

warrior *n.* 鬥士

vagabond *n.* 浪子

kaleidoscope *n.* 萬 花筒

歌曲出自迪士尼的經典動畫《獅子王》（*The Lion King*）。迷幻般的獅子故事、遼闊的非洲大草原，這一切很容易令人陶醉。這是一部充滿冒險和傳奇色彩的動畫片，是迪士尼的影片製作者們用他們的智慧和創造力，經過四年精雕細琢創造出來。

中文譯文

匆忙的一天漸入平靜
當翻滾的熱風
吹向遠方
那令人迷醉的時刻讓我心沉醉
永不停歇的鬥士啊
能夠和你在一起就已經知足

今夜，你可感受到我的愛
它與你我同在
好奇的遊者能與你同行
已經知足

今夜，你可感受到我的愛
它如此強烈
足使王子與遊子都堅信
愛是最美的力量

總有一天，每個人都會經歷
在這萬花筒般
變換的世界裏
狂野的天地蘊含着美好的韻律
落魄航海者的心
與你同鳴

（陳穎 譯）

精彩之處

wide-eyed：字面意義是「睜大眼睛的」，用來比喻好奇，天真無邪的表情。比如 wide-eyed innocence 就表示「天真爛漫」。

It's enough... best：這裏的王子代表了社會的上層人物，而浪子代表了社會的底層。「讓王子和浪子都相信」，實際是想表達全世界的人都相信。

star-crossed：表達的是「時運不濟」的意思，而用於兩個情人的時候，可以譯為「錯愛」。這句話來自星座占卜，表示一對情侶的本命星位置交錯，所以註定沒有好結果。曾有一部西班牙電影就以此命名。

歌詞中 day 和 away，rest 和 best，learn 和 turn，are 和 far 等兩兩押韻，結構上錯落有致，發音和諧動聽，給聽者帶來美感。

Candle in the wind (Goodbye England's Rose)
風中搖曳的燭光（再見英格蘭玫瑰）

Goodbye England's Rose
May you ever grow in our hearts
You were the **grace** that placed itself
Where lives were torn apart
You called out to our country
And you whispered to those in pain
Now you belong to heaven
And the stars spell out your name

And it seems to me you lived your life
Like a candle in the wind
Never fading with the sunset
When the rain set in
And your footsteps will always fall here
Along England's greenest hills
Your candle's burned out long before
Your **legend** ever will

Loveliness we've lost
These empty days without your smile
This torch we'll always carry
For our nation's golden child
And even though we try
The truth brings us to tears
All our words cannot express
The joy you brought us through the years

Goodbye England's Rose
From a country lost without your soul
Who'll miss the wings of your **compassion**
More than you'll ever know

**詞彙
註釋**

grace *n.* 優雅

legend *n.* 傳奇

compassion *n.* 同情

這首歌的作者是出身於英國皇家音樂學院，素有鋼琴怪傑、搖滾莫札特之譽的艾爾頓·約翰（Elton John）。1997 年，為紀念因車禍不幸罹難的戴安娜王妃而推出這首單曲。這張單曲唱片突破了 3180 萬張的銷量。

永別了，英格蘭的玫瑰
願你永遠盛開在我們心中
在生靈塗炭的地方
你獨自優雅地綻放
你喚起了國家的希望
你輕聲撫慰苦難中的人們
如今你已魂歸天堂
群星照耀着你的英名

你的一生
就像風中搖曳的燭光
即使大雨滂沱
你的光芒也永遠不會隨夕陽消失
你的足跡
遍佈英格蘭的青翠山岡
你的生命之燭雖早已燃盡
你的傳奇卻將永垂不朽

我們失去了你，可愛的人兒
沒有你微笑的日子空虛寂寞
我們將永遠高舉你手中的愛心火炬
紀念英格蘭敬愛的王妃
儘管我們強忍悲痛
你的離去仍讓我們聲淚俱下
千言萬語無法表達
這些年你帶給我們的歡樂

再見了，英格蘭玫瑰
你的離去讓整個國家都陷入了悲痛
你永遠都不會知道
我們將多麼懷念你的善良和仁慈

精彩之處

這裏用 England's Rose 來代表戴安娜王妃，她在英國人民的心目中是國寶。

torch：指用來照明天堂之路的火炬，人們希望戴安娜王妃一路走好。

（顏艷 譯）

▶ N O W   P L A Y I N G

Can't Help Falling in Love
情 不 自 禁 愛 上 你

英文
歌詞

Wise man says
Only fools rush in
But I can't help **falling in love with** you
Shall I stay
Would it be a sin
If I can't help falling in love with you

Like a river flows
Surely to the sea
Darling, so it goes
Some things are **meant to be**
Take my hand
Take my whole life too
For I can't help falling in love with you

Like a river flows
Surely to the sea
Darling, so it goes
Some things are meant to be

Ⅱ 詞彙
註釋

**fall in love with
someone** 愛上某人

meant to be 命中註
定

這首歌是貓王在電影《藍色夏威夷》（*Blue Hawaii*）裏演唱的經典情歌，收錄在電影原聲專輯裏。直到今日，貓王這位搖滾之王在世界樂壇仍然保持着無可爭議的統治地位。歌詞表達了對愛情熱情洋溢的渴望，如同夏日裏在驕陽下怒放的花朵。

中文譯文

智者説
傻瓜才沉迷戀愛
我偏偏情不自禁愛上你
我該留下嗎
這樣有罪嗎
如果我情不自禁愛上你

就像河流流淌
終將匯入海洋
親愛的，順其自然吧
人生就是這樣
緊握我手
掌握我一生
因為我已經情不自禁愛上你

就像河流流淌
終將匯入海洋
親愛的，順其自然吧
人生就是這樣

精彩之處

Wise man...rush in： 這句歌詞的意思是智者常說傻瓜才沉迷於戀愛。西方有句非常有名的俗語：love is blind（戀愛使人盲目／情人眼裏出西施）。此句中 fool 不是真的癡傻，而是指在戀愛時經常會為了對方做出一些可愛的傻事。

Like a river...sea： 它在文中表達的意思是我情不自禁愛上你彷彿是命運的指引，如同河流註定會注入大海般自然。

這首歌旋律優美動聽，配上貓王深情的演唱，成為經典的愛情歌曲。英語發音是否好聽除了掌握連讀略讀技巧外還取決於母音是否發音飽滿、到位。從歌曲中我們可聽到貓王不愧為底氣十足、母音飽滿的典範。

（李穎　譯）

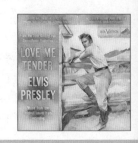

Love Me Tender
溫 柔 地 愛 我

英文
歌詞

Love me **tender**, love me sweet
Never let me go
You have made my life complete
And I love you so

Love me tender, love me true
All my dream **fulfill**
For my darling, I love you
And I always will

Love me tender, love me long
Take me to your heart
For it's there that I belong
And we'll never **part**

Love me tender, love me true
All my dream fulfill
For my darling, I love you
And I always will

Love me tender, love me dear
Tell me your are mine
I'll be yours through all the years
Till the end of time

詞彙
註釋

tender *adj.* 溫柔的

fulfill *v.* 實現

part *v.* 分開

這是「貓王」的電影《兄弟情深》（*Love Me Tender*）中的同名插曲。歌曲採用一把原聲結他伴奏，再加上「貓王」充滿磁性的嗓音和反覆的吟唱，成為經久不衰的名曲。電影原聲唱片在短短幾週就突破了 100 萬張的銷量，並在當年的 11 月登上了公告牌排行榜首位，蟬聯五週冠軍。

中文譯文

溫柔地愛我，甜蜜地愛我
永遠不要讓我走
你使我的人生更加完整
我是如此的愛你

溫柔地愛我，真心地愛我
我的夢想都實現
因為親愛的，我愛你
永遠愛着你

溫柔地愛我，永遠愛我
帶我到你心中
因為我屬於那裏
永遠不分離

溫柔地愛我，真心地愛我
我的夢想都實現
因為親愛的，我愛你
永遠愛着你

溫柔地愛我，深情地愛我
告訴我你屬於我
我將永遠屬於你
直到世界末日

（李音　譯）

 精彩之處

這首歌每段的語法結構基本相同。其突出的特點是每段前兩行都有一個 love me。每段中第一行的 love me 後面都是 tender，而第二行的 love me 後分別用不同的詞來描繪，即 sweet、true、long、dear。

第一段歌詞講述愛與人生的關係，愛使人生變得完整，圓滿；第二段講述愛與理想，愛可以使人夢想成真；第三段談到愛的歸屬；第四段主人公表達了愛的誓言。這四段歌詞概括了愛的基本特徵：溫柔、甜蜜、忠誠、永恆和深情。

Only Time
唯有時光

 英文歌詞

Who can say where the road goes
Where the day flows
Only time
And who can say if your love grows
As your heart chose
Only time

Who can say why your heart sighs
As your love flies
Only time
And who can say why your heart cries
When your love dies
Only time

Who can say when the roads meet
That love might be in your heart
And who can say when the day sleeps
If the night keeps all your heart
Night keeps all your heart

Who can say if your love grows
As your heart chose
Only time
And who can say where the road goes
Where the day flows
Only time
Who knows
Only time
Who knows
Only time

這首歌來自愛爾蘭著名歌手恩雅（Enya），收錄在她 2000 年發行的專輯《無雨的一天》（*A Day Without Rain*）中。她憑藉這張專輯斬獲當年的「年度最暢銷新世紀藝人」、「年度最暢銷女藝人」和「年度最暢銷愛爾蘭藝人」三項重量級獎項，該專輯還獲得第 44 屆格林美「最佳新世紀專輯獎」。

 中文譯文

誰能説出，路向哪個方向延伸
時光又往哪裏流淌
唯有時光
誰能説出，內心愛的強弱增減
是否真如心之所向
唯有時光

誰能説出，愛若早已散為塵埃
為何心還不停歎息
唯有時光
誰能説出，愛若隨風枯萎凋零
為何心卻依然啜泣
唯有時光

誰能説出，兩條路若在此交匯
愛已埋藏心底
誰能説出，白晝若已昏然沉睡
黑夜是否蔓延心底
充斥心靈每寸土地

誰能説出，內心愛的強弱增減
是否真如心之所向
唯有時光
誰能説出，道路將朝哪裏延展
時光又往哪裏流淌
唯有時光
誰能領悟
唯有時光
誰能領悟
唯有時光

（李穎 譯）

 精彩之處

the day sleeps：此處使用的是擬人和借代的手法，將時間擬人化。

這首歌簡潔樸實，卻蘊含着深刻的哲理。歌詞更是將押韻運用到了極致，如 go 和 flow 以及 grow，sighs 和 cries 及 flies，meet 和 heart 等，構成豐富的韻腳，讀來朗朗上口，體現了音韻美。

Eric Clapton

My Father's Eyes
父 親 的 眼 睛

英文
歌詞

Sailing down behind the sun
Waiting for my prince to come
Praying for the healing rain
To restore my soul again

Just a **toerag** on the run
How did I get here
What have I done
When will all my hopes arise
How will I know him
When I look into my father's eyes
My father's eyes

Then the light begins to shine
And I hear those ancient **lullabies**
And as I watch this **seedling** grow
Feel my heart starts to overflow

Where do I find the words to say
How do I teach him
What do we play
Bit by bit, I've realized
That's when I need my father's eyes.

**詞彙
註釋**

toerag *n.* 惡 棍 (俚
語)

lullaby *n.* 搖籃曲

seedling *n.* 幼苗

jagged *adj.* 參差不齊
的

Then the **jagged** edge appears
Through the distant clouds of tears
I'm like a bridge that was washed away
My foundations were made of clay

As my soul slides down to die
How could I lose him
What did I try
Bit by bit, I've realized
That he was here with me
I looked into my father's eyes

這首歌取自艾力‧克萊普頓（Eric Clapton）的專輯《天路歷程》（*Pilgrim*）。克萊普頓曾經獲得過 19 座格林美獎。2003 年在《滾石》雜誌評選的 100 大結他手中，他位列第四。第 41 屆格林美獎評選中，他憑這歌獲最佳流行男歌手獎。

中文譯文

日落前起航
等待我的王子到來
祈求治癒傷痛的雨露
再次喚醒我的靈魂

就像一個亡命之徒
我是怎樣來到這世間的
我到底做了甚麼
我何時才能看到希望
我怎樣才能瞭解他
當我深情地望着父親的眼睛
父親的眼睛

我看到他閃爍的目光
我彷彿聽到了那古老的搖籃曲
當我看着這個幼小的生命茁壯成長
我心中父愛洋溢

我該對他說甚麼
我該怎麼教導他
我該怎麼陪他玩耍
漸漸地，我意識到
我多麼需要看到父親雙眼

然後陡峭的海角出現了
穿越遙遠的淚雲
我就像一座被沖毀的橋
我的根基由泥土造成而已

當我的靈魂墮落消亡
我怎麼能失去他
我到底做了甚麼
漸漸地，我意識到
他始終都與我在一起
我深情地望着父親的眼睛

（顏艷 譯）

 精彩之處

這首歌的創作源於克萊普頓本人的親身經歷，他從來沒有見過自己的父親。歌曲中還提到了他早年夭折的兒子，表達了他失去父親和兒子的痛苦，以及希望享有父愛和給予父愛的熱切願望。

Waiting for my prince to come：把父親比作自己的王子，表達父親在他心中的高大偉岸形象。

Where...paly：通過一次次的追問，表達了克萊普頓因缺少父愛而不知如何向自己的兒子表達父愛的困惑和遺憾。

Wonderful Tonight
美 妙 今 夜

It's late in the evening
She's wondering what clothes to wear
She puts on her make-up
And brushes her long blond hair
And then she asks me: "Do I look all right?"
And I say: "Yes, you look wonderful tonight."

We go to a party
Everyone turns to see
This beautiful lady
Is walking around with me
And then she ask me: "Do you feel all right?"
And I say: "Yes, I feel wonderful tonight."

I feel wonderful because I see
The love light in your eyes
And wonder of it all
That you just don't realize
How much I love you

It's time to go home now
And I've got an aching head
So I give her the car keys
And she helps me to bed
And then I tell her
As I turn off the light
I say: "My darling, you are wonderful tonight."
Oh my darling, you are wonderful tonight

這歌是英國歌手艾力·克來普頓（Eric Clapton）的經典之作，收錄於他的專輯《緩慢的手》（Slowhand）中。克來普頓是 20 世紀最成功的音樂家之一，他曾獲得過 19 座格林美獎，也是史上唯一一位曾三度入主搖滾名人堂的搖滾傳奇人物。現在，這曲已成為西方舞會和婚禮的一個必備曲目。

中文譯文

夜色已濃
她還在為如何打扮猶豫不決
她化好妝
輕梳那頭金色的長髮
轉過身來問我：「我看起來還好吧？」
我答道：「很好，你今晚看起來美極了。」

我們去參加派對
所有人都轉過頭來，欣賞
這位美麗的女士
正與我並肩行走
她問我：「感覺還好嗎？」
我說道：「是的，我今晚感覺好極了。」

我感覺好極了，是因為我看見
你眼中愛的光芒
而且我一直在想
你可能還沒發現
我有多麼愛你

該是回家的時候了
我卻頭痛得厲害
我把車鑰匙交給她
她把我扶上床
我告訴她
在我把燈關掉的時候
我說：「親愛的，你今晚美極了。」
噢，親愛的，你今晚真的美極了。

精彩之處

light：作者用 light 一詞，生動準確地傳達了「愛的光芒」。

這首歌創作於 1976 年的一個晚上，克來普頓在等他未婚妻時創作了這首歌。該歌曲講述的就是從等待到赴宴再到返回的這樣一個美妙夜晚。

（楊爽　蔣夢陽　譯）

Fool's Garden
▶ N O W   P L A Y I N G

Lemon Tree
檸檬樹

I'm sitting here in a boring room
It's just another rainy Sunday afternoon
I'm wasting my time, I got nothing to do
I'm hanging around, I'm waiting for you
But nothing ever happens, and I **wonder**

I'm driving around in my car
I'm driving too fast, I'm driving too far
I'd like to change my point of view
I feel so lonely, I'm waiting for you
But nothing ever happens, and I wonder

I wonder how, I wonder why
Yesterday you told me about the blue-blue sky
And all that I can see is just a yellow lemon tree
I'm turning my head up and down
I'm turning, turning, ... around
And all that I can see is just another lemon tree

I'm sitting here, I miss the power
I'd like to go out taking a shower
But there's a heavy cloud inside my head
I feel so tired, put myself into bed
Where nothing ever happens, and I wonder

Isolation is not good for me
Isolation, I don't want to sit on a lemon tree
I'm stepping around in a **desert** of joy
Maybe anyhow I get another toy
And everything will happen, and you wonder

I wonder how, I wonder why
Yesterday you told me about a blue-blue sky
And all that I can see is just a yellow lemon tree

**詞彙
註釋**

wonder *v.* 納悶

desert *n.* 沙漠

《檸檬樹》一歌由傻子的花園樂隊（Fool's Garden）於 1996 年首唱。這首單曲使這支原本籍籍無名的德國 5 人樂隊一下子紅遍歐洲和亞洲。歌曲被翻譯成 40 多種語言，唱片的銷量超過 600 萬張。

中文譯文

我獨坐在無聊的房間
又一個有雨的星期天下午
我無所事事，打發着時間
我不安地徘徊，等待着你到來
但你終究沒有到來，我很納悶

我開着我的車
怎料開得太快，走得太遠
我想換個角度看世界
卻仍感到寂寞，等待着你到來
但你終究沒有到來，我很納悶

我不知如何，不知為何
昨天你給我描繪那藍藍的天空
但我所看見的只有一棵金黃的檸檬樹
我上下打量
我四處張望
卻只看見另一棵檸檬樹

我呆坐着，無精打采
我想去洗個澡
卻揮不去心裏的陰雲
我筋疲力盡，把自己扔到床上
但你終究沒有到來，我很納悶

自我封閉，可不適合我
自我封閉，我可不想獨坐在檸檬樹上
我在歡愉的沙漠中漫步
或許我能找到新的玩具
甚麼都會發生，你很納悶吧

我不知如何，不知為何
昨天你跟我描繪那藍藍的天空
我所能看見的只是那金黃的檸檬樹

（宋思怡 譯）

精彩之處

a heavy cloud：這裏的 cloud 雖譯為陰雲，但實指的是「我」沮喪的心情——在這樣一個無聊的午後，天陰沉沉的，而「我」卻沒有等來我的戀人，只好獨坐在房間裏發呆，心裏的煩悶自然難以排遣，揮之不去。

put myself into bed：把自己扔到床上，「扔」這一動作既表現「我」的無精打采，又生動活潑，更符合少女的心理特點。

Glen Hansard & Marketa Irglova

Falling Slowly
緩 慢 降 落

I don't know you
But I want you
All the more for that
Words fall through me
And always fool me
And I can't react

And games that never amount
To more than they're meant
Will play themselves out

Take this sinking boat and point it home
We've still got time
Raise your hopeful voice
You have a choice
You've made it now

Falling slowly, eyes that know me
And I can't go back
Moods that take me and **erase** me
And I'm painted black

Well, You have suffered enough
And **warred with** yourself
It's time that you won

Take this sinking boat and point it home
We've still got time
Raise your hopeful voice
You have a choice
You've made it now

Falling slowly sing your melody
I'll sing along
I paid the cost too late

**詞彙
註釋**

erase v. 擦去

war with 同……進行
爭鬥

這是愛爾蘭音樂電影《一奏傾情》（Once）中的插曲，由愛爾蘭音樂人葛蘭·漢塞德（Glen Hansard）和捷克女孩瑪可塔·伊爾格洛娃（Marketa Irglova）創作並演唱，二人同時也是電影的男女主角。該歌曲獲得第 80 屆奧斯卡原創歌曲獎。

中文譯文

雖然我對你一無所知
但是卻想和你在一起
想要更深入地瞭解你
想說的話卻說不出口
讓我就像個傻瓜一般
不知道該如何回應你

遊戲就只是遊戲而已
別無意義
終有一天將會要結束

乘上這艘將要沉的船，給它指明回家的路吧
我們還有時間
揚起你的希望之聲
你還有選擇的權利
現在你做出了選擇

閉上洞悉我的雙眼
我已經無法自拔了
憂傷吞噬了我
我被黑暗覆蓋

你歷經了磨難
你與自己交戰
你贏得了勝利

乘上這艘將要沉的船，給它指明回家的路吧
我們還有時間
揚起你的希望之聲
現在你做出了選擇
你現在可以做到

慢慢唱出你的旋律
我將和你一同吟唱
我雖付代價卻為時已晚（現在的你早已經離開我）

（王孜　譯）

精彩之處

fall through：在這歌中是指想說的話無法表達出口。

And games...meat：never...more than 是「從不會超越……」的意思，因而此句之意即為「遊戲僅僅是遊戲而已」。

play out：是「結束，做完」的意思，而此處的 themselves 指的是前文中的「遊戲」，所以此句的意思是指遊戲終究會有結束的一天。

painted black：此處指作者受到悲傷情緒的影響，被黑暗吞噬，整個世界變得不見天日。

Glenn Medeiros

Nothing's Gonna Change My Love for You
此 情 永 不 移

If I had to live my life without you near me
The days would all be empty
The nights would seem so long
With you I see forever oh so clearly
I might have been in love before
But it never felt this strong
Our dreams are young and we both know
They'll take us where we want to go

Hold me now
Touch me now
I don't want to live without you

Nothing's gonna change my love for you
You oughta know by now how much I love you
One thing you can be sure of
I'll never ask for more than your love

Nothing's gonna change my love for you
You oughta know by now how much I love you
The world may change my whole life through
But nothing's gonna change my love for you

If the road ahead is not so easy
Our love will lead a way for us
Just like a guiding star
I'll be there for you if you should need me
You don't have to change a thing
I love you just the way you are
So come with me and share the view
I'll help you see forever too

這首歌曾風靡全球，原來的版本由爵士樂手 George Benson 演繹。1987 年，美國的葛倫·麥德羅斯（Glenn Medeiros）憑藉他優美的嗓音和英俊的外表，將本曲捧紅。香港歌手呂方也曾將之改編成粵語歌《求你講清楚》。

中文譯文

如果我必須過着沒有你的生活
日子會變得空虛
夜晚會變得漫長
有你在，我能如此清晰地看到未來
也許我曾愛過
但從未像現在這樣強烈
我們都知道，我們的夢想充滿活力
能指引我們到嚮往的地方

抱緊我
撫摸我
我不想過沒有你的生活

沒有甚麼能改變我對你的愛
你現在應該知道我愛你有多深
你可以確信一點
除了你的愛，我別無所求

沒有甚麼能改變我對你的愛
你現在應該知道我愛你有多深
世界可以徹底改變我的一生
但沒有甚麼能改變我對你的愛

如果前方的道路並不平坦
愛會引領我們向前
像啟航的明星一樣
我會等候在你需要我的地方
你毋須做任何改變
我就是愛你現在的樣子
陪着我，我們一起分享眼前的風景
我也會幫你看到永恆

（劉媛媛 譯）

精彩之處

這首歌通過真摯而精妙的詞曲和歌者的深情演繹，唱出了男女主人翁對對方的強烈思念。

Gloria Gaynor

I Will Survive
我 會 活 下 去

英文
歌詞

At first I was afraid I was **petrified**
Kept thinking I could never live without you by my side
But then I spent so many nights
Thinking how you did me wrong
And I grew strong
And I learn how to get along

And so you're back from outer space
I just walked in to find you here with that sad look upon
your face
I should have changed that stupid lock
I should have made you leave your key
If I'd known for just one second you'd back to bother me

Go on now, go walk out the door
Just turn around now
'Cause you're not welcome anymore
Weren't you the one who tried to hurt me with goodbye
Did I **crumble**
Did I lay down and die

Oh no, not I, I will survive
Oh, as long as I know how to love I know I'll stay alive
I've got all my life to live
I've got all my love to give and I'll survive

It took all the strength I had not to fall apart
Kept trying hard to mend the pieces of my broken heart
And I spent oh so many nights
Just feeling sorry for myself
I used to cry
But now I hold my head up high

And you see me somebody new
I'm not that chained up little person still in love with you
And so you felt like droppin' in
And just expect me to be free
But now I'm savin' all my lovin' for someone who's
lovin'me

■■ 詞彙
註釋

petrified *adj.* 不知所
措

crumble *v.* 崩潰

這首歌由美國 70 年代「的士高女王」格洛麗亞·蓋納（Gloria Gaynor）演唱。1979 年該曲連續六週蟬聯冠軍白金曲，成為當時的士高的必備歌曲，1980 年這首歌更獲得了格林美獎史上唯一一個「最佳的士高錄音」大獎，之後多次被用於電影插曲。

 中文譯文

起初我很害怕，不知所措
我總是想，身邊沒有你我一定活不下去
但後來，我花了很多個夜晚
去想你是如何辜負了我
然後，我變得堅強
學會了獨立

然而，你又從外面回來
當我走進門時
發現了滿臉愁容的你
我早該換掉那該死的鎖
我早該叫你把鑰匙留下
如果我早知道你會回來騷擾我的話

滾吧！滾出這扇門
給我馬上轉身離開
你已經不受歡迎
你就是那個用手來傷害我的傢伙
我會崩潰嗎
我會坐以待斃嗎

哦！不，我會活下去
一旦我學會如何去愛，我就能活下去
我會好好地過一生
我會用全部的愛去奉獻，我會活下去

我用盡全身力氣，不讓自己崩潰
我努力修補着自己破碎的心
我花了多個夜晚
為自己感到難過
難過的哭泣
但現在的我昂首闊步

你看到的我已經脫胎換骨
我不再是那個被枷鎖困住的愛情小白痴
你今天突然來找我
說希望我自由的屁話
我現在可是把我的愛完完整整地保留給
那個愛我的人了

（張玉嬌 譯）

 精彩之處

1978 年春，格洛麗亞在歐洲登台時不小心跌落舞台，致使脊髓受損並因此臥床達 9 個月之久，更為不幸的是復健期間母親去世，一連串的打擊幾乎讓她崩潰。康復後格洛麗亞努力振作，寫下這首歌以證明自己戰勝了怯懦。

do sb. wrong：原意是「冤枉、委屈某人」，在這裏指「辜負某人」。

just... to find：表示「發現」，但含有出乎意料的意思。

Goo Goo Dolls

Iris
彩虹女神

英文
歌詞

And I'd give up forever to touch you
'Cause I know that you feel me somehow
You're the closest to heaven that I'll ever be
And I don't want to go home right now

And all I can taste is this moment
And all I can breathe is your life
'Cause sooner or later it's over
I just don't want to miss you tonight

And I don't want the world to see me
'Cause I don't think that they'd understand
When everything's made to be broken
I just want you to know who I am

And you can't fight the tears that ain't coming
Or the moment of truth in your lies
When everything seems like the movies
Yeah you bleed just to know you're alive

And I don't want the world to see me
'Cause I don't think that they'd understand
When everything's made to be broken
I just want you to know who I am

這首另類搖滾歌曲是電影《天使之城》（*City of Angels*）的原聲音樂，由美國著名搖滾樂隊咕咕娃娃（Goo Goo Dolls）演唱。憑藉這首歌，樂隊獲得 1999 年第 41 屆格林美「年度歌曲」、「年度唱片」和「最佳流行演唱團體」三項大獎提名。著名歌手艾薇兒·拉維妮（Avril Lavigne）十分鍾情這歌，將它作為自己婚禮上的舞曲。

我願意放棄永生只為撫摸你
我相信你定會感知我的存在
我希望能像你一般如此接近天堂
此時此刻的我不想回到來時的路

我只想細細品味這一刻
深情感受你生命的氣息
這一切終有結束的瞬息
我只想珍惜今夜的你

不願意被世人看見
因為他們不會瞭解
即使萬物終歸毀滅
也要你知道我是誰

你不能忍住還未流下的淚
抑或是謊言中真實的片刻
當一切如電影片段般閃過
你用獻血來證明你的存在

不願意被世人看見
因為他們不會瞭解
即使萬物終歸毀滅
也要你知道我是誰

（葛婷婷　譯）

精彩之處

When everything's…I am： 這是整首歌的高潮，也是真諦之所在。作者知道世間萬事萬物終究要化為虛有。

21Guns
２１響禮炮

英文
歌詞

Do you know what's worth fighting for
When it's not worth dying for
Does it take your breath away
And you feel yourself **suffocating**
Does the pain weigh out the pride
And you look for a place to hide
Did someone break your heart inside
You're in ruins

One, 21 guns
Lay down your arms
Give up the fight
One, 21 guns
Throw up your arms into the sky, you and I

When you're at the end of the road
And you lost all sense of control
And your thoughts have **taken their toll**
When your mind breaks the spirit of your soul
Your faith walks on broken glass
And the hangover doesn't pass
Nothing's ever built to last
You're in ruins

Did you try to live on your own
When you burned down the house and home
Did you stand too close to the fire
Like a liar looking for **forgiveness** from a stone

When it's time to live and let die
And you can't get another try
Something inside this heart has died
You're in ruins

Ⅱ 詞彙
註釋

suffocate *v.* 窒息

take toll 造成傷害

forgiveness *n.* 寬恕

這首另類搖滾歌曲由深受美國朋克音樂風格影響的綠日樂隊（Green Day）創作並演唱，並且延續了他們上一張專輯的風格，再次表達了反對戰爭、希冀和平的主題思想，同時安慰了對美國政府失望透頂的美國民眾。這首歌多次被用於美國電影、電視劇插曲，其高亢深情的旋律很能瞬間打動人心。

中文譯文

你知道何事值得奮戰嗎
當它不值得為其犧牲
它讓你窒息嗎
你也感覺窒息
是否痛苦壓倒了驕傲
你也尋找藏身之處
可曾有人讓你心碎
使你只剩下殘骸

鳴炮，21 響
放你武器
停止廝殺
鳴炮，21 響
讓我們把武器拋向天空吧

當你窮途末路時
當你行屍走肉時
當你想着喪鐘敲響時
當你的心智磨滅了靈魂的精華
信念毫無依靠
宿醉的迷失依然縈繞
沒有甚麼永恆
你只剩殘骸

當焚滅家園時
可曾想過為自己而活
可曾玩火自焚
傻瓜般向石頭苦求寬恕

到了生死關頭
你沒有了重新選擇的機會
你心中已喪失了些東西
你只剩殘骸

（張楠 譯）

精彩之處

在美國的國葬中以及重大的紀念節日中需要由軍人鳴槍 21 響。鳴槍 21 響是很有政治意味的。本歌曲中「鳴槍 21 響」表達的是對結束戰爭的期待。

at the end of the road：
指參戰士兵心理上窮途末路的窘境。

stone：在這句話中，可以把 stone 理解為墓碑，以表達對戰爭中受害者的哀悼。

▶ N O W P L A Y I N G

Boulevard of Broken Dreams
碎 夢 大 道

I walk a lonely road
The only one that I have ever known
Don't know where it goes
But it's home to me and I walk alone

I walk this empty street
On the **boulevard** of broken dreams
Where the city sleeps
And I'm the only one and I walk alone
I walk alone

My **shadow's** the only one that walks beside me
My shallow heart's the only thing that's beating
Sometimes I wish someone out there will find me
Till then I walk alone

I'm walking down the line
That divides me somewhere in my mind
On the border line
Of the edge and where I walk alone

Read between the lines
What's fxxked up and everything's alright
Check my vital signs
To know I'm still alive and I walk alone
I walk alone

My shadow's the only one that walks beside me
My shallow heart's the only thing that's beating
Sometimes I wish someone out there will find me
Till then I walk alone

II 詞彙
註釋

boulevard *n.* 大道

shadow *n.* 影子

這首另類搖滾歌曲是綠日樂隊（Green Day）的經典歌曲。這首歌來自專輯《美國偶像》（*American Idiot*），專輯封面上畫着淌血的手榴彈。綠日樂隊將對現今社會、媒體混亂現象的不滿，在歌曲中充分地呈現出來。這張專輯曾榮獲 2005 年美國 MTV 八項提名，獲得七項大獎。

 中文譯文

我走在孤獨的路上
我唯一記得的路上
不知去向何方
但這是我的歸宿我的路

我走在空無一人的街上
在碎夢大道上
城市陷入沉睡
我獨自一人行走
我孤獨地行走

只有影子與我相伴
只有虛弱的心臟還在跳動
有時我希望有人找到我
不然我只有孤獨地走下去

我一直走在
那割裂我思想的路上
在邊界線上
我孤獨地行走

思索着
混亂與理智的界限
檢查我的心跳
我還活着，我孤獨地行走
我孤獨地行走

只有影子與我相伴
只有虛弱的心臟還在跳動
有時我希望有人找到我
不然我只有孤獨地走下去

（宋思怡 譯）

 精彩之處

My shadow's...me： 表現出一種極度孤獨的狀態，與整首歌的關鍵字 lonely 十分契合。

Read between the lines： 原意為「體會言外之意」，這句話省略了主語 I，意思是「在碎夢大道上孤獨地思考」。

vital signs： 原意為「脈搏，呼吸，體溫等生命體徵」，為了與前文 shallow heart 相呼應，因此將這句話譯為「檢查我的心跳」。

Guns N' Roses

Sweet Child O' Mine
我 可 愛 的 孩 子

She's got a smile that it seems to me
Reminds me of childhood memories
Where everything was as fresh as the bright blue
sky
Now and then when I see her face
She takes me away to that special place
And if I **stared** too long
I'd probably break down and cry

Oh, sweet child o' mine
Oh, oh, oh, oh, sweet love of mine

She's got eyes of the bluest skies
As if they thought of rain
I hate to look into those eyes
And see an **ounce** of pain
Her hair reminds me of a warm safe place
Where as a child I'd hide
And pray for the thunder
And the rain
To quietly pass me by

Oh, sweet child o' mine
Oh, oh, oh, oh , sweet love of mine
Oh, oh, oh, sweet child o' mine
Oh, oh ,oh, sweet love of mine

Where do we go
Where do we go now

**詞彙
註釋**

now and then 偶爾

stare *v.* 凝視

ounce *n.* 少量

這首歌來自於美國硬搖滾樂隊槍炮與玫瑰（Guns N'Roses）。這是他們的第三支單曲，一經發行便成為公告牌榜單的冠軍歌曲。這是由樂隊主唱艾克賽爾·羅斯（Axl Rose）作詞，寫給女友的情歌。很多著名歌手和樂隊都曾翻唱這歌。這歌的結他伴奏被很多音樂組織評為最佳結他伴奏。

 她彷彿是在對我甜甜地笑
兒時的記憶頓時湧起
一切如同藍天般
清澈皎皎
每次她出現在我面前
都會把我帶回到那裏
我如果久久地凝望着
我會崩潰，會不由地哽咽

啊，我可愛的孩子
啊，我甜美的愛情

她雙眼如湛藍的天
彷彿將要淚如雨下
我不忍凝望她的雙目
看到她一絲的傷楚
她的秀髮讓我記起個溫暖安全的地方
小時候，我會躲在那裏
祈禱着雷鳴
祈禱着暴雨
靜靜地離我而去

啊，我可愛的孩子
啊，我甜美的愛情
啊，我可愛的孩子
啊，我甜美的愛情

我們要去往何處
我們現在要去往何處

（葛婷婷 譯）

 **精彩
之處**

She...special place： 在這裏 place 並不是某個具體的地方，而是個虛指的概念，指小時候能夠帶給「我」無限歡樂與溫馨的地方。

And pay...me by： 這裏將雷鳴與暴雨擬人化，主人翁祈禱它們能夠靜靜地離他而去，生動俏皮地表達了希望自己能夠躲過這些惡劣的天氣。

You're Beautiful
你 是 這 麼 美

My life is **brilliant**
My love is pure
I saw an angel
Of that, I'm sure
She smiled at me on the subway
She was with another man
But I won't lose no sleep on that
'Cause I've got a plan

You're beautiful it's true
I saw your face in a crowded place
And I don't know what to do
'Cause I'll never be with you

Yeah she caught my eye
As we walked on by
She could see from my face that I was fxxking high
And I don't think that I'll see her again
But we shared a moment that will last till the end

You're beautiful, it's true
I saw your face in a crowded place
And I don't know what to do
'Cause I'll never be with you

You're beautiful, it's true
There must be an angel with a smile on her face
When she thought up that I should be with you
But it's time to face the truth
I will never be with you

詞彙
註釋

brilliant *adj.* 卓越的

2005 年的夏天，占士·布蘭特（James Blunt）憑藉自己的第三張單曲《你是這麼美》（*You're Beautiful*）一舉成名。憂鬱的嗓音加上憂鬱的曲調成就了這首歌曲的成功。一經推出，這首歌就佔據了英國單曲榜的第 4 位，後更是連續 5 次榮獲英國單曲榜冠軍，更蟬聯了全球 5 大排行榜的冠軍。演唱者布蘭特同時也是這首歌的詞曲作者。

中文 譯文

我的生活如此美好
我的愛如此純真
我遇見過一個天使
對此，我深信不疑
在地鐵上她對我微微一笑
雖然她和一個男人相伴
不過我不會因此輾轉難眠
因為我早有準備

你這麼美 這千真萬確
人潮擁擠中我瞥見你的臉
我卻茫然不知所措
因為你我註定不會相守相依

是的，她佔據了我的視線
在我們擦肩而過的時候
她能從我的臉上看到我的欣喜若狂
我想我再也不會遇見她了
但我們擁有了永恆的瞬間

你這麼美，這千真萬確
人潮擁擠中我瞥見你的臉
我卻茫然不知所措
因為我不能與你相隨

你這麼美，這千真萬確
她的臉上必有天使在微笑
天使一定也認為我們應該在一起
現在我要面對現實
我不能與你相隨

（楊亞男　譯）

精彩 之處

Of that, I'm sure： 此 處 that 指代的是上一句的「我看見了天使」。

I won't lose no sleep on that： 此處為雙重否定，但並非用以肯定，而是強調否定，意為我不會因此失眠以致輾轉反側。

she caught my eye： 這裏隱喻為「她吸引了我」。

walk on by： 兩人擦身而過，意指兩人並不相識，匆匆走過，卻不打招呼

James Morrison

You Make It Real
成為現實

So much **craziness** surrounding me
So much going on it gets hard to breathe
All my faiths has gone
You bring it back to me
You make it real for me

Well, I'm not sure of my **priorities**
I've lost site of where I'm meant to be
And like holy water washing over me
You make it real for me

And I'm running to you baby
You are the only one who saves me
That's why I've been missing you lately
'Cause you make it real for me

When my head is strong but my heart is weak
I'm full of **hurricanes** and **uncertainty**
But I can find the words
You teach my heart to speak
You make it real for me

Everybody's talking in words I don't understand
You got to be the only one
Who knows just who I am
And you shine in the distance
I hope I can make it through
Because the only place
That I want to be is right back home with you

I guess there's so much more have to learn
But if you're here with me
I know which way to turn
You always give me somewhere
Somewhere I can learn
You make it real for me

詞彙 註釋

craziness *n.* 瘋狂

priority *n.* 優先權

hurricane *n.* 感情爆發

uncertainty *n.* 捉摸不定

這首輕柔搖滾歌曲由英國歌手占士·莫里森（James Morrison）演唱，收錄在其 2008 年 9 月發行的專輯《歌曲給你，真相給我》（*Songs for You, Truths for Me*）中。占士·莫里森從一個普通的洗車工成為當時最成功、最受矚目的樂壇新人。

中文譯文

周圍一切如此瘋狂
重壓之下喘氣困難
全部信念都已破滅
是你把我的夢追回
將我夢想變為現實

無法確定生活重心
我已失去生活方向
你如那聖水滌蕩我
將我夢想變為現實

我要奔向親愛的你
只有你才能解救我
我一直在思念着你
你讓我的夢想成真

外表堅強內心軟弱
感情爆發喜樂無常
但我已經開始領悟
你教我用心去說話
你讓我的夢想成真

別人的話我聽不懂
你才是唯一的那個
真正知曉我心的人
你是燈塔照亮遠方
我盼望着我能成功
我唯一想要的地方
就是與你一起回家

成長的道路還很長
但是若和你在一起
我知道該前往何方
你一直指引我方向
讓我能夠從中學習
你讓我的夢想成真

（李穎 譯）

精彩之處

And like... for me：耶穌出世時，聖靈從天而降，落在他身上。於是基督徒認為讓新生嬰兒接受聖水浸泡，可以洗去污垢和罪孽，讓靈魂變得純潔。此處將女孩比喻成聖水洗滌了他的靈魂，拯救了他的世界，表明了內心對女孩的萬分感激。

Jason Mraz

► N O W P L A Y I N G

93 Million Miles
9 3 0 0 萬 英 里

英文
歌詞

93 million miles from the Sun
People get ready, get ready
Because here it comes it's a light
A beautiful light, over the **horizon** into your eyes
Oh, my how beautiful
Oh, my beautiful mother
She told me: Son in life you're gonna go far
And if you do it right you'll love where you are

Just know, wherever you go
You can always come back home

240 thousand miles from the Moon
We've come a long way to belong here
To share this view of the night
A **glorious** night
Over the horizon is another bright sky
Oh, my how beautiful
Oh, my **irrefutable** father
He told me: Son sometimes it may seem dark
But the absence of the light is a necessary part

Every road is a **slippery** slope
There is always a hand you can hold on to
Looking deeper through the telescope
You can see that the home's inside of you

Ⅱ 詞彙
註釋

horizon *n.* 地平線

glorious *adj.* 極好的

irrefutable *adj.* 不可
駁倒的，堅強不屈的

slippery *adj.* 滑的

這首歌出自有「男巫」之稱的美國創作歌手——傑森·瑪耶茲（Jason Mraz）2012 年的專輯《愛就一個字》（*Love is a Four Letter Word*）。傑森以其強大的現場演唱功力聞名樂壇，是第 52 屆格林美獎最佳流行男歌手得主。

太陽之遙，9300 萬英里
人們快快準備吧
光芒就要普照
聖美陽光，就要劃躍地平線
多麼美好
就像我慈愛的母親
她曾對我說：人生之路，萬里跋涉
只要腳下無歧途，心中就有無限愛

無論去往何方
家人永遠等待你歸來

月亮之遙，24 萬英里
千里迢迢，我們相聚於此
共用良辰美景
夜色溫柔
嶄新一天即將來到
多麼靜默
就像我堅強的父親
他曾對我說：人生之路，總有黯淡
磨練在所難免

每條路上都有可能跌倒
但總會有機遇可以把握
尋望內心深處
家從未離開

精彩之處

Son in life...far：對 go far 的理解不必局限於「要遠離家鄉」，本句重在 in (the whole) life，指整個人生中，會有很長的路要走，很多的選擇要做，目光不能止於眼前。

A glorious...sky： over the horizon 是「即將來臨，初現端倪」的意思，bright sky 與 glorious night 相呼應，指夜色褪去，白天將近。

absence of the light：即「迷失方向」或「黯淡消沉」。

（趙瑋 譯）

► N O W P L A Y I N G

Sweet Dreams
夢 天 堂

The shadows are **waltzing**
The moon beams are calling
Like a dream I am falling into
Silver **threads** lined with dew
Twinkling stars seem to shine just for you

Behind your eyes
Are endless blue skies
You travel places I want to come, too
Each breath that you breathe
Is a brush stroke that leads me to you

So sleep
Fall into night's **indigo hue**
Believe me, it's true
There's nothing that I would not do
For my dream is sweet dreams for you

It seems far away
But there once was a day
It was grey in a world without you
To this heart like a dove from above
The miracle of your love found me

So hush you bye
And don't you cry
Sweetly dream, little baby

Yes, sleep
Lose yourself in night's indigo hue
Believe me, it's true
There's nothing that I would not do
For my dream is sweet dreams for you

⏸ 詞彙
註釋

waltz *v.* 跳華爾滋舞

thread *n.* 線

indigo *adj.* 靛藍色的

hue *n.* 色彩

這歌是珠兒所發行的一張搖籃曲風專輯中的經典名曲。珠兒的演唱生涯光環無數，曾獲三項格林美獎提名、全美音樂獎和 MTV 音樂錄影帶獎。她因長年致力於慈善活動而被《魅力》（*Glamour*）雜誌十周年版評選為「年度風雲女性」。

翩翩起舞的華爾滋
月色美如斯
童話夢中現
水珠兒滴答串銀線
星星只對你眨眼笑

遙遠那地方
看不盡藍天
想追隨你的腳步
你的一舉一動
我都心心念念

睡吧睡吧
在溫柔夜色的懷抱
所有美好真實環繞
我會為你做好一切
只願你美夢香甜

似乎遙不可及
曾有那麼一天
沒你陪伴，了無生趣
你像天使落入人間
喚醒我全部心愛

輕輕說聲晚安
寶貝乖乖安睡
進入甜甜夢鄉

睡吧睡吧
在溫柔夜色的懷抱
所有美好真實環繞
我會為你做好一切
只願你美夢香甜

（趙瑋 譯）

 **精彩
之處**

The moon...calling：
moon beams 指「月光傾瀉」，而 calling 為「召喚」之意，在此以擬人的修辭手法將傾城月色賦予了靈動的生命。

Behind your eyes： 眼睛後面，即看不到的遙遙天際。

The miracle...me：
miracle 不是指「奇跡般的愛」，而是引申為「為孩子的愛超越一切，無與倫比」。

So hush you bye： 這是一首搖籃曲，say bye 是「道聲晚安」的意思。

Joan Baez

Donna Donna
多娜，多娜

英文歌詞

On a **wagon** bound for market
There's calf with a **mournful** eye
High above him there's a swallow
Winging swiftly through the sky
How the winds are laughing
They laugh with all their might
Laugh and laugh the whole day through
And half the summer's night
Donna Donna Donna Donna

Stop complaining, said the farmer
Who told you a calf to be
Why don't you have wings to fly with
Like the swallows so proud and free
How the winds are laughing
They laugh with all their might
Laugh and laugh the whole day through
And half the summer's night
Donna Donna Donna Donna

Calves are easily bound and **slaughtered**
Never knowing the reason why
But whoever treasures freedom
Like the swallow has learned to fly
How the winds are laughing
They laugh with all their might
Laugh and laugh the whole day through
And half the summer's night
Donna Donna Donna Donna

⏸ 詞彙註釋

wagon *n.* 馬車

mournful *adj.* 悲哀的

slaughter *v.* 屠殺

這首歌由美國民謠女皇瓊·貝茲（Joan Baez）演唱。她曾發行過八張黃金專輯，六次獲得格林美獎提名。不僅在音樂上才華橫溢，她更是以一顆博愛的心受到世人的尊敬與愛戴，她是一名嚮往和平的鬥士。此曲秉承了一貫的音樂風格，沒有嬌柔造作，有的只是一把木結他，自然中流露着清新，簡單中透着純美。天生絕妙的嗓音會令你過耳難忘。

一輛趕集的馬車上
有一頭眼神哀傷的小牛
高處一隻飛燕
在藍天中翱翔
風兒在開懷地笑
笑得如此起勁
從黎明笑到黃昏
笑到仲夏夜之半
多娜，多娜，多娜，多娜

農夫說不要抱怨
誰叫你是一頭牛
你為何不能展翅飛翔
像燕子一樣驕傲而自由
風兒在開懷地笑
笑得如此起勁
從黎明笑到黃昏
笑到仲夏夜之半
多娜，多娜，多娜，多娜

小牛任人束縛和屠宰
卻從不知為何
嚮往自由的人們
要像燕子一樣學會飛翔
風兒在開懷地笑
笑得如此起勁
從黎明笑到黃昏
笑到仲夏夜之半
多娜，多娜，多娜，多娜

（葛婷婷 譯）

 精彩之處

多娜是一名女子的名字，她象徵被壓迫的女性，歌曲中提到的一些名詞也各有象徵意義，牛象徵被壓迫者，燕子象徵自由的人，農夫象徵當權者。

But whoever...fly： 這句歌詞的意思為「像燕子一樣珍視自由的人們要學會飛翔」，鼓勵人們衝破壓迫，追求自由。

歌詞巧妙地運用了押韻技巧，如 night 和 might，eye、sky、fly 和 why 等，變換的尾韻使發音豐富和諧，朗朗上口，同時也增添了音韻美和文體美。

John Denver

Take Me Home, Country Road
鄉村路，帶我回家

英文
歌詞

Almost heaven, West Virginia
Blue Ridge Mountains, Shenandoah River
Life is old there
Older than the trees
Younger than the mountains
Growing like a **breeze**

Country roads take me home
To the place I belong
West Virginia, Mountain Momma
Take me home, country roads

All my memories, gather round her
Miner's Lady
Stranger to blue water
Dark and dusty
Painted on the sky
Misty taste of moonshine
Teardrops in my eyes

Country roads, take me home
To the place I belong
West Virginia, Mountain Momma
Take me home, country roads

I hear her voice in the morning hours
She calls me
The radio reminds me of my home far away
And driving down the road
I get a feeling
That I should have been home
Yesterday , yesterday

Country roads, take me home
To the place I belong
West Virginia, Mountain Momma
Take me home, country roads

⏸ 詞彙
註釋

Blue Ridge Mountains 藍嶺山脈（在西維吉尼亞）

breeze *n.* 微風

misty *adj.* 朦朧的

teardrop *n.* 淚滴

演唱者約翰·丹佛（John Denver）曾獲 21 次金唱片獎和 4 次白金唱片獎。此曲是其成名作，曲調深情、悠揚，長短句搭配錯落有致、自然和諧。歌詞中所呈現的故鄉那純樸、熟悉的種種意向，與歌者通過重複部分所表現的遊子歸心似箭之情完美地結合在一起。整首歌唱起來一氣呵成，思鄉之情表現得淋漓盡致。

中文譯文

天堂般的西維吉尼亞
藍嶺山脈山，納多河流
那兒生靈悠遠
比樹木古老
比大山年輕
如微風般生生不息

鄉村路，帶我回家吧
回到我屬於的地方
西維吉尼亞，大山媽媽
鄉村路，帶我回家

我所有的思念都縈繞着她
礦工的妻子
從未見過大海
黑灰與塵土
籠罩在空中
月色朦朧
我的雙眼飽含淚水

鄉村路，帶我回家吧
回到我屬於的地方
西維吉尼亞，大山媽媽
鄉村路，帶我回家

清晨我聽見她的聲音
在呼喚着我
收音機使我想起了遠方的家
開車駛過公路
心中有種感覺
我就該回家
昨天，昨天

鄉村路，帶我回家吧
到我生長的地方
西維吉尼亞，大山媽媽
鄉村路，帶我回家吧

（李音 譯）

精彩之處

Growing like a breeze：
該句運用了比喻的修辭手法，指自然界萬物生靈如清風般徐徐生長。

Dark and dusty：因為西維吉尼亞是美國著名的產煤州，所以在歌詞中描繪了被煤灰煙塵籠罩的天空。鄉村歌曲一向把務農、礦工和伐木當做受人尊敬的職業，認為他們身上體現了美國人兢兢業業、自我奮鬥的價值觀。

should have done sth.：
意為「本該發生而實際上未發生的事情」。這句話表達了歌者的思鄉和歸心似箭之情。

John Denver

Perhaps Love
或 許 愛 如 此

英文
歌詞

Perhaps love is like a **resting** place
A **shelter** from the storm
It exists to give you comfort
It is there to keep you warm
And in those times of trouble
When you are most alone
The memory of love will bring you home

Perhaps love is like a window
Perhaps an open door
It invites you to come closer
It wants to show you more
And even if you lose yourself
And don't know what to do
The memory of love will see you through

Oh, love to some is like a cloud
To some as strong as steel
For some a way of living
For some a way to feel
And some say love is holding on
And some say letting go
And some say love is everything
And some say they don't know

Perhaps love is like the ocean
Full of **conflict**, full of Pain
Like a fire when it's cold outside
Or **thunder** when it rains
If I should live forever
And all my dreams come true
My memories of love will be of you

詞彙
註釋

resting *adj.* 休息的

shelter *n.* 避難所

conflict *n.* 矛盾

thunder *n.* 雷

這歌原唱為美國歌手約翰·丹佛（John Denver），旋律優美清新，歌詞溫暖動人，一度受到多位著名歌手的青睞，先後加以翻唱。

中文譯文

愛，或許是避風塘
遠離風雨飄搖
永存一份舒適
久駐一片溫暖
低谷的歲月中
寂寞肆虐交織
愛的記憶將心歸置

愛，或許是一扇窗
亦是未封之門
召喚你去靠近
希望給你更多
即使迷失自我
彷徨無措
愛的記憶帶你走過

哦，有些人的愛，如雲易消散
有些人的愛，似鋼不可斷
有人重方式
有人重感覺
有人說，愛要堅持不懈
有人說，愛要懂得放棄
有人說，愛是世間一切
有人還說，愛是難以名狀

愛，或許是大海
矛盾洶湧，滿載痛苦
也如烈火燃燒，吞噬嚴寒
還似雨中驚雷
如果過盡我一生
所有夢想都實現
愛的記憶全是你

（趙瑋 譯）

精彩之處

resting place：在此處強調了愛給人帶來的安全感與放鬆感。

like a cloud：此處的 cloud 與下句的 steel 形成對比，強調的是愛情柔弱的一面。

For some...feel：way of living 和 way of feel 在曲中表達的是，愛情對於有些人而言用於填充或完成生活的一個方面，對另一些人而言，是借助愛情感受世界，感受人情冷暖。

John Lennon

Imagine
想 像（理 想 世 界）

Imagine there's no heaven
It's easy if you try
No hell below us
Above us only sky
Imagine all the people
Living for today

Imagine there's no countries
It isn't hard to do
Nothing to kill or die for
And no religion too
Imagine all the people
Living life in peace

You may say I'm a dreamer
But I'm not the only one
I hope someday you'll join us
And the world will be as one

Imagine no **possessions**
I wonder if you can
No need for greed or hunger
A brotherhood of man
Imagine all the people
Sharing all the world

 詞彙
註釋

possession *n.* 佔有

這首世界級的經典曲目，出自英國著名樂隊披頭四（The Beatles）靈魂人物約翰·連儂（John Lennon）的同名專輯。2002 年英國廣播公司民調顯示，連儂在有史以來最偉大的 100 位英國人物評選中排名第 8。這一單曲在公告牌排行榜中最高升至第 3 位，而同名專輯則雄踞專輯榜榜首。

中文譯文

想像如果沒有天堂
這很容易，不妨一試
下面沒有地獄
上面只有蒼穹
想像所有的人
都活在當下

想像如果國家不存在
這很容易，不妨一試
沒有殺戮或犧牲
也沒有宗教
想像所有的人
都活在和平世界

你可能說我在做夢
但我不是唯一一個
希望有一天，你加入我們
那時世界將成為一家

想像沒有獨佔
對你來說，這不容易
不再貪婪，沒有飢餓
四海皆兄弟
想像所有的人
分享着整個世界

（喬楠 譯）

精彩之處

作為一個和平主義者的連儂，在這首歌中想要表達的是對和平世界的憧憬和嚮往，根據這一意思，把這歌的名字 Imagine 譯為「理想世界」可能更為貼切。

religion：曾有人說，世界上的任何宗教一開始時都有着好的願望，但最後總是被瘋狂的人所異化。連儂本人是一個很看重精神世界的人，他不是反對精神世界的宗教，而是反對「有組織的宗教」（Organized Religion），只是歌詞需要簡潔押韻，不適合用 Organized Religion。

Leona Lewis

Lovebird
愛情鳥

II will lay down next to you
Stay in bed all afternoon
We were birds of a **feather**
We were always together
And I never will forget
All the little things you said
And that beautiful summer, used to call me a love bird

But the time went on, the wait is blown, and I have gone
And a scar that I feel in
And my wings have been broken

And I can't believe
That I would ever want to be set free
But I just can't stay

So your lovebird's flyin' away
Your lovebird's flyin' away away
Is my heart's been stuck in a cage
I sing my song, so pretty
Dum, dum, diddy
And I miss you every day
But there's nothing left to say
Gotta sing my song, so pretty, dum dum diddy

I want the world in my feet
Even if it's **bittersweet**
Wanna stand on my own and
Put my heart in my own hands
'Cause I've began to see that you and me are different
breeds
So I gotta believe in
Gotta get back to breathing

And you'll always be a part of me
You made me who I am
But I gotta say I'm not afraid to test my wingspan
'Cause it seems when you love something
Let it go, let it go, open up the gate
Your lovebird's flying away

詞彙
註釋

feather *n.* 羽毛

bittersweet *adj.* 苦
樂參半的

breed *n.* 品種

李奧娜・路易絲（Leona Lewis）於 2008 年被評為「最佳新人」，在美國權威榜單公告牌上創下多項紀錄。這歌出自李奧娜第 3 張專輯《心心相了》（Glassheart）。歌曲 MV 中，李奧娜彷彿化身一隻愛情鳥，在籠中掙扎，婉轉而讓人心碎。

中文譯文

躺在你身旁
陪你到天荒
我們是同林之鳥
形影相隨，永不分離
難以忘懷
你的隻言片語
那個美麗夏日，你喚我愛情鳥

時光流逝，等待不再，我已離去
內心傷痕纍纍
羽翼折斷

難以相信
我曾渴望離開，重獲自由
但是我已無法停留

你的愛情鳥已飛走
你的愛情鳥已飛去
我的心囚於牢籠
獨自吟唱，如此美麗
噠噠滴滴
日日思念
卻無言以表
獨自吟唱，如此美麗，噠噠滴滴

我要俯視世界
即使有苦有樂
我要獨自獨立
掌控自我命運
我已發現
你我並非同林鳥
我要堅定信念
重新自由呼吸

你永遠是我的一部分
你造就了現在的我
但我已不再畏懼飛翔
因為當你愛上一個人
就要學會放手，打開大門
你的愛情鳥要展翅高飛

精彩之處

the wait is blown： 化無形為有形，wait 本是一種無形的東西，這裏被風吹散，與前面的 the time went on 主動句式形成對比，刻畫了女主角苦等無果的無奈。

Is my heart's been stuck in a cage： 運用暗喻的手法，cage 代指情感的束縛，這裏將其形象化，給聽眾以豐富的想像空間，同時也與前面的 lovebird 相呼應。

（黃靈燕 譯）

Lionel Richie

Say You Say Me
說 出 你 的 心 聲 ， 說 出 我 的 心 聲

英文
歌詞

Say you, say me
Say it for always
That's the way it should be
Say you, say me
Say it together naturally

I had a dream, I had an **awesome** dream
People in the park
Playing games in the dark
And what they played was a masquerade
But from behind the walls of doubt
A voice was crying out

Say you, say me
Say it for always
That's the way it should be
Say you, say me
Say it together naturally

As we go down life's lonesome highway
Seems the hardest thing to do
Is to find a friend or two
That helping hand someone who understands
And when you feel you've lost your way
You've got someone there to say
I'll show you oo, oo, oo

So you think you know the answers
Oh no
Well the whole world's got ya dancing
That's right I'm telling you
It's time to start believing
Oh yes
Believe in who you are
You are a shining star oh

❚❚ 詞彙
註釋

awesome *adj.* 可 怕
的

Say you, say me
Say it for always
That's the way it should be
Say you, say me
Say it together naturally

這首慢搖滾歌曲是電影《白夜逃亡》（*White Night*）的主題曲，由萊昂納爾·里奇（Lionel Richie）譜寫，同時由其擔任主唱。這歌作為主題曲享譽世界。

說出你的心聲，說出我的心聲
彼此坦誠到永久
一切本該如此
說出你的心聲，說出我的心聲
大家一起暢所欲言

我做了一個夢，一個可怕的夢
人們在公園裏
躲藏在陰暗的角落裏玩遊戲
他們玩着假面舞會
在猜疑的高牆後面
一個聲音在大喊

說出你的心聲，說出我的心聲
彼此坦誠到永久
一切本該如此
說出你的心聲，說出我的心聲
大家一起暢所欲言

我們走在人生寂寞的高速路上
似乎最難的
莫過於有一兩個知己
一兩個幫你懂你的知己
在你迷失方向的時候
他們會在那裏對你說
我給你指引

也許你認為已知曉答案
不，不
世界讓你變得瘋狂
這正是我要告訴你的
重新建立信任的時候到了
對，是的
相信自己
你是一顆閃耀的星

說出你的心聲，說出我的心聲
彼此坦誠到永久
一切本該如此
說出你的心聲，說出我心聲
大家一起暢所欲言吧

精彩之處

masquerade：象徵人與人之間互不信任的狀態。戴着假面的舞者們熱鬧地跳舞，卻各懷心思。每個人都好像戴着面具生活，把真實的自己掩藏在最黑暗的角落。

the walls of doubt：用高牆來形容人與人之間的隔膜，充分表現了人際關係的疏離與冷漠。

歌曲旋律悠揚動聽，配上歌手充滿激情的演唱，成為經久不衰的金曲。歌詞也很好地運用了押韻技巧，如 me 和 be，park 和 dark，doubt 和 out 等，豐富的尾韻使發音富有層次感，聲音和諧動聽。

（宋思怡　譯）

Louis Armstrong

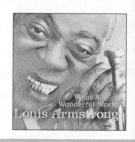

▶ NOW PLAYING

What a Wonderful World
多 麼 美 好 的 世 界

I see trees of green
Red roses too
I see them **bloom** for me and you
And I think to myself
What a wonderful world

I see skies of blue and clouds of white
The bright blessed day
The dark **sacred** night
And I think to myself
What a wonderful world

The colors of the rainbow
So pretty in the sky
Are also on the faces of people going by
I see friends shaking hands saying
"How do you do"
They're really saying "I love you"

I hear babies crying
I watch them grow
They'll learn much more than I'll ever know
And I think to myself
What a wonderful world

 詞彙
註釋

bloom *v.* 開花

sacred *adj.* 神聖的

這首歌是路易士·阿姆斯壯（Louis Armstrong）在 1967 年發行的單曲，發行後在英國取得很大成功，成為當年英國單曲排行榜的冠軍，1968 年仍然是英國最熱賣的單曲，66 歲的路易士·阿姆斯壯也因這首歌成為當時最高齡的單曲排行榜冠軍歌手。他對於爵士樂的重要意義，就好像古典音樂的巴赫、搖滾樂的貓王，是爵士樂史上永恆的靈魂人物。

中文譯文

我看見綠色的樹木
還有紅色的玫瑰
它們為你我綻放
於是我告訴自己
多麼美好的世界

我看見了藍色的天空，白色的雲朵
白天明亮美好
夜晚安靜神聖
於是我告訴自己
多麼美好的世界

繽紛的彩虹
在天空中那麼絢麗
照映在行人的臉上
我看見朋友們
握手問候
那是在說「我愛你們」

我聽見嬰兒的哭泣
也見證他們的成長
他們將會學習很多東西，遠遠超出我的水準
於是我告訴自己
多麼美好的世界

（王晶 譯）

**精彩
之處**

I see...too：歌詞很簡單，寥寥數語，對生活隨處可見的景象（綠樹、紅花、藍天、白雲、彩虹、哭泣的嬰兒等）的描繪，卻道出對美好世界的熱愛，可見詞作者內心的安然與平和，浮躁的現代都市人缺少的不正是這種發現美好世界的心態嗎？

I hear...grow：這裏運用了兩個感官動詞 hear 和 watch，但後面跟的動詞形式不一樣，感官動詞後接動詞 ing 形式往往表示正在發生的行為，而後接動詞原形則表示行為發生的全過程。

這首歌旋律優美，歌詞簡潔，加上演唱者飽含深情的演唱，具有強烈的感染力。歌詞中 grow 和 know，sky 和 by，以及 night 和 white 等兩兩押韻，讀來朗朗上口。

Don't Cry for Me Argentina
阿根廷，別為我哭泣

It won't be easy
You'll think it strange
When I try to explain how I feel
That I still need your love
After all that I've done

You won't believe me
All you will see
Is a girl you once knew
Although she's dressed up to the nines
At sixes and sevens with you

I had to let it happen
I had to change
Couldn't stay all my life down at heel
Looking out of the window
Staying out of the sun
So I chose freedom
Running around trying everything new
But nothing impressed me at all
I never expected it too

Don't cry for me Argentina
The truth is I never left you
All through my wild days
My mad existence
I kept my promise
Don't keep your distance

And as for fortune and as for fame
I never invited them in
Though it seemed to the world
They were all I desired
They are **illusions**
They're not the **solutions**
They promise to be
The answer was here all the time
I love you and hope you love me

Have I said too much?
There's nothing more I can think of to say to you
But all you have to do is look at me to know
That every word is true

illusion *n.* 幻象

solution *n.* 解決方法

這首歌首次亮相於 1978 年倫敦愛德華劇院上演的著名音樂劇《貝隆夫人》（Evita）。該音樂劇講述了阿根廷前第一夫人貝隆的傳奇一生。1996 年麥當娜在電影版中演唱這曲。該電影曾獲三項金球獎。

中文譯文

那不會容易
你會覺得奇怪
當我要表達我的感受時
我說我仍需要你的愛
在我犯下諸多錯誤以後

你不會相信我
你眼裏的我
總是那個你從前認識的女孩
她打扮得優雅得體
卻無法與你相稱

我必須要讓你相信
我必須改變
我不能潦倒一生
永遠眺望着窗外
不見天日
所以我選擇自由
我四處奔波，不斷嘗試
但卻沒有絲毫收穫
我也從未想過結果會如此

阿根廷，請別為我哭泣
事實上，我從未離開你
在我狂野的歲月中
瘋狂的經歷裏
我仍信守諾言
請不要將我拒諸門外

財富和名望
我從未追逐
儘管全世界都認為
這正是我所渴望的
但他們只是水月鏡花
不是解決之道
不是他們承諾的靈丹妙藥
我的回答從未改變
我愛你啊，希望你也愛我

我是否說得太多了？
我再沒有想到甚麼可對你說
但是，你需要做的就是看着我
知道每一個字都是真的

（張旋 譯）

精彩之處

At sixes...you：此處「你」指的是阿根廷。年齡在此是一種具體化的隱喻修辭，是一種口語化的表達方法，通過直接的對比表達了對祖國的熱愛、忠誠和謙恭。

down at heel：意為「鞋履後跟破損的」，代指「衣衫襤褸」，即「潦倒」。

impress：原意為「留下印象」，此處指我在「四處奔波，不斷嘗新」中並沒有獲得收穫。

illusions 和 solutions 在這首歌中有相反的意思，即「鏡花水月」和「解決之道」。同時兩個表語在句末構成尾韻押韻。

Mariah Carey

▶ NOW PLAYING

Hero
英 雄

There's a hero
If you look inside your heart
You don't have to be afraid
Of what you are
There's an answer
If you reach into your soul
And the sorrow that you know
Will melt away

And then a hero comes along
With the strength to carry on
And you cast your fears aside
And you know you can survive
So when you feel like hope is gone
Look inside you and be strong
And you'll finally see the truth
That a hero lies in you

It's a long road
When you face the world alone
No one reaches out a hand
For you to hold
You can find love
If you search within yourself
And the **emptiness** you felt
Will disappear

Lord knows
Dreams are hard to follow
But don't let anyone
Tear them away
Hold on there will be tomorrow
In time
you'll find the way

詞彙
註釋

emptiness *n.* 空虛

瑪麗亞·凱莉因其 2 億多張的唱片銷量和無數的音樂榜單記錄，以及 5 個八度的高亢音域和洛可哥式的演唱技巧聞名於世。這歌是《音樂盒》（*Music Box*）專輯中的第二支單曲，也是瑪麗亞的代表作。此曲曾給予無數人力量。

中文譯文

有一個英雄
如果你探尋內心
你不必害怕
自己是甚麼樣的人
有一個答案
如果你深入自己的靈魂
你所經歷的痛苦
將煙消雲散

一個英雄向你走來
充滿力量，執着前行
你把恐懼拋開
知道自己能挺過去
所以當感到希望破滅
回歸本心，保持堅強
最終將看到
心中住着一個英雄

漫漫長路
當獨自面對世界
沒有人伸出手
讓你緊握
一定能發現愛
如果審視內心
心中的空虛
將不復存在

天知道
夢想難以追求
但是別讓任何人
把夢奪走
堅持住，還會有明天
最終
你將會找到自己的路

（楊璐　譯）

精彩之處

look inside your heart： 此處翻譯為「探尋內心」，後文中的 reach into your soul，search within yourself 均表示此意。

melt away： 原指雪的「融化」，此處譯為「煙消雲散」。

survive： 原為「倖存，存活」，此處譯為「挺過去」。

It's a long road： 譯為「漫漫長路」，此處用到了暗喻的修辭手法，「漫漫長路」並非指現實中的路，而是指人生的道路。

Mariah Carey

Without You
不 能 沒 有 你

No I can't forget this evening or your face as you were leaving
But I guess that's just the way the story goes
You always smile, but in your eyes
Your sorrow show
Yes, it shows

No I can't forget tomorrow
When I think of all my sorrow
When I had you there but then I let you go
And now it's only fair that I should let you know
What you should know

I can't live
If living is without you
I can't live
I can't give anymore

Well, I can't forget this evening or your face as you were leaving
But I guess that's just the way the story goes
You always smile
But in your eyes
Your sorrow shows
Yes, it shows

此歌由英國歌手哈利‧尼爾森（Harry Nilsson）原唱。瑪麗亞翻唱此曲，並收錄於她 1993 年的專輯《音樂盒》（*Music Box*）中。當時正值尼爾森去世，該單曲在英國登上單曲榜第一名，這也是她在英國榜上僅有的兩首冠軍單曲之一。

 中文譯文

我無法忘記這個美妙的夜晚
以及你離去時的臉龐
但是我猜想這才是故事的結局
你總是微笑，但是在你的眼裏
卻流露哀傷
沒錯，那是哀傷

我無法忘記明日
當我想起我所有的悲痛
我擁有了你，最後卻又選擇放棄你
現在我只是想讓你知道
一些你該知道的事情

如果沒有你
我無法活下去
我無法活下去
我再也無法付出

我無法忘記這個美妙的夜晚
以及你離去時的臉龐
但是我猜想這才是故事的結局
你總是微笑
但是在你的眼裏
卻流露着哀傷
沒錯，那是哀傷

（王海僑 譯）

 精彩之處

No I can't... goes： 此句一經出口，即帶來整首歌濃濃的哀傷。歌詞表達了因為愛人的離去而感到悲痛不已，加上凱莉富有質感的歌聲，迅速地將人們帶入歌曲的畫面中。

I can't live... anymore： 這幾句是歌曲中的副歌部分，歌者將滿腔情感都傾注在這幾句看似簡單的歌詞上，表達了一種當事人想對愛人傾訴真情的感情。

這首歌旋律優美，歌詞中也包含豐富的尾韻，如 evening 和 leaving，sorrow 和 tomorrow，go 和 know 等，節奏感加強，發音和諧悅耳，使聽眾產生強烈的共鳴。

Michael Jackson

Beat It
躲 開

英文
歌詞

They told him
Don't you ever come around here
Don't wanna see your face, you better disappear
The fire's in their eyes and their words are really clear
So beat it, just beat it

You better run, you better do what you can
Don't wanna see no blood, don't be a **macho** man
You wanna be tough, better do what you can
So beat it, but you wanna be bad

Just beat it, beat it, beat it
No one wants to be defeated
Showin' how **funky** and strong is your fight
It doesn't matter who's wrong or right
Just beat it, beat it

They're out to get you
Better leave while you can
Don't wanna be a boy
You wanna be a man
You wanna stay alive
Better do what you can
So beat it, just beat it
You have to show them that you're really not scared
You're playin' with your life
This ain't no truth or dare
They'll kick you, then they beat you
Then they'll tell you it's fair

⏸ 詞彙
註釋

macho *adj.* 大男子氣
概的

funky *adj.* 膽戰心驚
的

這首歌由美國已故著名流行歌手，被譽為「流行音樂之王」的米高積遜（Michael Jackson）演唱，收錄在其 1982 年專輯的《戰慄》（*Thriller*）中。他憑藉這歌獲得第 26 屆格林美最佳搖滾男歌手，成就他流行音樂史上不朽的傳奇。

中文譯文

他們警告他
看你還敢來這兒
別讓我再看見你，趕緊消失了
他們眼中，怒火熊熊，吐出的話也很沖
那就躲開吧，躲得遠遠的

趕快跑吧，最好拼盡全力
不想見血，就別去逞英雄氣
你想要充好漢，現實先把你壓彎
所以躲開吧，但你偏迎險而上

躲開吧，躲開，快躲開
沒人甘當敗寇
都在瘋狂狠鬥
對錯只是藉口
乾脆躲開吧，躲得遠遠的

他們衝過來抓你
三十六計走為上計
不承認乳臭未乾
你想做個男子漢
但還是保命要緊
做自己力所能及
還是躲開吧，躲開
你想告訴他們你毫不畏懼
你這是在玩命兒
無關乎真理或勇氣
他們會踢你、扁你
然後告訴你暴力即是正義

精彩之處

beat it：這個詞是美國俚語，字面意思是「打它」，實則是「躲開」的意思。整首歌都在以激昂的語調不斷重複這個詞，流露出激烈而好鬥的情緒，表達的卻是呼籲青少年不要用暴力解決問題的主題，演唱方式與歌曲內涵的反差更讓人印象深刻。

整首歌詞都是以第二人稱的方式演繹，有許多類似忠告的話語，或責怪，或勸阻，很能打動人心。

（劉紫薇　譯）

Michael Jackson

Heal the World
拯 救 世 界

英文
歌詞

There's a place in your heart
And I know that it is love
And this place could be much
Brighter than tomorrow
And if you really try
You'll find there's no need to cry
In this place you'll feel
There's no hurt or sorrow
There are ways to get there
If you care enough for the living
Make a little space
Make a better place

Heal the world
Make it a better place
For you and for me
And the entire human race
There are people dying
If you care enough for the living
Make it a better place
For you and for me

If you want to know why
There's love that cannot lie
Love is strong
It only cares of joyful giving
If we try we shall see
In this **bliss** we cannot feel

米高積遜獲得過格林美終身成就獎，3 次入選搖滾名人堂，並獲得多個健力士世界紀錄。他擁有 15 座格林美獎、26 座全美音樂獎、17 首美國公告牌排行榜冠軍單曲。這歌於 1991 年發行，是一首呼喚世界和平的歌曲，歌詞倡導人們保護和珍惜環境，讓戰爭遠離。

你心中有一方淨土
那裏滋生愛的種子
這個地方
絢爛更勝明天
你若已經努力
就無需再哭泣
在這個地方
苦痛與悲傷都已不在
總有方法到達這裏
只要你心懷生者
營造一些空間
勾勒一個更美好的地方

拯救世界
讓它更加美好
為了我和你
為了全人類
每時每刻都有人離開這個世界
倘若你心懷生者
就請創造一個美好的世界
為了我和你

如果你想要尋一個理由
有一種愛不會說謊
愛是強大的
愛只是快樂的付出
用心嘗試就會領悟
心中有愛

Fear or dread
We stop existing and start living
Then it feels that always
Love's enough for us growing
Make a better world, make a better world

And the dream we would conceived in
Will reveal a joyful face
And the world we once believed in
Will shine again in grace
Then why do we keep strangling life
Wound this earth, crucify it's soul
Though it's plain to see, this world is heavenly
Be God's glow

We could fly so high
Let our spirits never die
In my heart I feel you all are my brothers
Create a world with no fear
Together we'll cry happy tears
See the nations turn their swords into plowshares
We could really get there
If you cared enough for the living
Make a little space to make a better place

 詞彙
註釋

bliss *n.* 極樂

就不會恐懼
我們不再是活着，而是開始真正的生活
然後，那感覺將持續下去
愛足夠我們成長
創造一個更美好的世界，創造一個更美好的世界

我們構思中的夢想
將展露喜悅的面貌
我們曾經信賴的世界
會在祥和中再次閃耀
然而，我們為何仍在扼殺生命
傷害了地球，處死其靈魂
雖然這很容易明白
這世界天生就是上帝的榮光

我們可以在高空飛翔
讓我們的精神不滅
在我心中，我感到你我都是兄弟
共同創造一個沒有恐懼的世界
我們一起流下喜悅的淚水
看着許多國家把刀劍變成了犁
我們真的可以做到
如果你真心關懷生者
營造一些空間，創造一個更美好的地方

（葛婷婷　譯）

 精彩之處

We stop... living：existing 指的是「行屍走肉般的活着，人生毫無意義」，living 指的是「珍視生命，享受生活」。

Michael Jackson

You Are Not Alone
你 不 孤 單

英文
歌詞

Another day has gone
I'm still all alone
How could this be
You're not here with me
You never said goodbye
Someone tell me why
Did you have to go
And leave my world so cold

Everyday I sit and ask myself
How did love slip away
Something whispers in my ear and says
That you are not alone
For I am here with you
Though you're far away
I am here to stay

You are not alone
For I am here with you
Though we're far apart
You're always in my heart
You are not alone, all alone why oh

Just the other night
I thought I heard you cry
Asking me to come
And hold you in my arms
I can hear your prayers
Your burdens I will bear
But first I need your hand
Then forever can begin

Everyday I sit and ask myself
How did love slip away
Something whispers in my ear and says
That you are not alone
For I am here with you
Though you're far away
I am here to stay

Whisper the words
Then I'll come running
And I
And, girl, you know that I'll be there
I'll be there

這首歌是米高積遜於 1995 年發行的專輯《歷史》（*History*）中的第二支單曲，該曲發行首週就奪得了美國流行單曲榜冠軍。該曲在歐洲各國音樂榜上也連獲佳績，至今仍廣受歡迎，被普遍認為是他最傑出的作品之一。

中文譯文

又一天過去
我依舊孤單
怎麼會這樣
因你不在我身旁
你從沒說再見
有人告訴我原因
你必須走嗎
我的世界一片淒涼

每天我坐下來問自己
愛怎會遠離
耳邊傳來低語
你並不孤單
我會與你相伴
儘管你遠在天邊
我會在此等待

你並不孤單
因我在此相伴
儘管我們遠隔天涯
你總在我心間
你並不孤單

那天夜裏
我想我聽到你在哭泣
你呼喚我快來
將你擁入我懷裏
我聽到你的祈願
我願承受你的重擔
但先要執子之手
方能天長地久

每天我坐下來問自己
愛怎會遠逝
耳邊傳來低語
你並不孤單
我在此與你相伴
儘管你遠在天邊
我會在此等待

悄悄說出那三個字
我將飛奔而來
和我
女孩啊，你知道我會在這裏
常在你身邊

（郭曉芹　譯）

精彩之處

Another day has gone, I'm still all alone：歌曲一開始便奠定了舒緩、憂傷的基調，並開門見山地唱出該曲的關鍵字 alone。這首歌是一首關於愛情和分隔的 R&B 歌謠。

歌中有許多尾韻的使用，如 goodbye、why 和 cry，stay 和 away，apart 和 heart 等，或以雙母音結尾，發音飽滿拉長，或以爆破音結尾，發音急促有力，和諧動聽，引起聽眾強烈的共鳴。

Mike Oldfield(Dana Winner)

Moonlight Shadow
月 影 下 的 祈 禱

英文
歌詞

The last that ever she saw him
Carried away by a moonlight shadow
He passed on worried and warning
Carried away by a moonlight shadow
Lost in the riddle last Saturday night
Far away on the other side
He **was caught in** the middle of a desperate fight
And she couldn't find how to push through

The trees that whisper in the evening
Carried away by a moonlight shadow
Sing a song of sorrow and grieving
Carried away by a moonlight shadow
All she saw was a **silhouette** of a gun
Far away on the other side
He was shot six times by a man on the run
And she couldn't find how to push through

I stay, I pray
I see you in heaven far away
I stay, I pray
I see you in heaven one day

4 a.m. in the morning
Carried away by a moonlight shadow
I watched your vision forming
Carried away by a moonlight shadow
Stars move slowly in a silvery night
Far away on the other side
Will you come to talk to me this night
But she couldn't find how to push through

Far away on the other side
Caught in the middle of a hundred and five
The night was heavy and the air was alive
But she couldn't find how to push through

⏸ 詞彙
註釋

be caught in 被捲入

silhouette *n.* 輪廓

這首歌是英國作曲家麥克·歐菲爾德（Mike Oldfield）的不朽之作，最早收錄於他的專輯《危機》（*Crisis*）中。該曲於 1983 年問世，相傳為紀念披頭四被槍殺的主音連儂而作。丹娜·雲妮（Dana Winner）演唱的版本則收錄於其專輯《永誌難忘》（*Unforgettable*）中。

中文譯文

那是她最後一次見他
浸潤在溶溶月影中
帶着憂慮和警示
浸潤在溶溶月影中
消失在上週六晚的謎團中
在那遠遠的河對岸
他捲入了一場慘烈的戰鬥
她不知所措

夜晚樹林呢喃
浸潤在溶溶月影中
淺唱着悲傷的挽歌
浸潤在溶溶月影中
她看到槍的輪廓
在那遠遠的河對岸
他被一個逃跑的人射中六槍
她不知所措

我止步祈禱
希望能在遙遠的天國看到你
我止步祈禱
希望終有一天在天國看到你

凌晨四點鐘
浸潤在溶溶月影中
我彷彿看到你的身影
浸潤在溶溶月影中
銀色的夜幕群星慢移
從那遠遠的河對岸
今晚你是否還會來跟我説説話
她不知所措

在那遠遠的河對岸
悼念的人群圍繞着他
夜色凝重，空氣也在哽咽
他不知所措

（張旋 譯）

精彩之處

carried away by... shadow：此句用擬人化的手法表達月影將愛人帶走，體現一種傷心、無助的心情。

Sing a...and grieving：意為「樹林低語，淺唱着悲傷的挽歌」。這種擬人化的手法渲染出夜晚的靜謐和哀傷。sing、song、sorrow 三個單詞押頭韻；這句話貫穿了始終，反復吟詠，有旋律之美。

I Wanna Be Free
我渴望自由

I wanna be free
Like the **bluebirds** flying by me
Like the waves out on the blue sea
If your love has to tie me
Don't try me
Say good-bye

I wanna be free
Don't say you love me say you like me
But when I need you beside me
Stay close enough to guide me, **confide in** me

I wanna hold your hand
Walk along the sand
Laughing in the sun
Always having fun
Doing all those things
Without any **strings**
To tie me down

I wanna be free
Like the warm September wind, babe
Say you'll always be my friend, babe
We can make it through the end, babe
Again, babe, I gotta say
I wanna be free

**詞彙
註釋**

bluebird *n.* 青鳥

confide in 信賴

string *n.* 束縛

這首歌出自門基樂隊（The Monkees）1966 年發行的同名專輯。門基樂隊是 20 世紀 60 年代美國知名組合，當時他們的唱片銷量超過了貓王和披頭四樂隊，是當時全球最受歡迎的流行樂隊。該歌曲於 1967 年在一些國家以單曲形式發佈。2010 年，香港電影《歲月神偷》使用此曲作為電影插曲。

中文譯文

我渴望自由
如青鳥側畔飛翔
如海浪拍打沙灘
如果你的愛會將我束縛
請不要愛我
說再見吧

我渴望自由
請不要說你愛我，只說喜歡我吧
若我需要你在我身邊
請靠近我指引我相信我

我渴望牽着你的手
沿着海岸漫步
在太陽下歡笑
永遠這樣快樂
做愛做的事
隨心而行
無拘無束

我渴望自由
如那九月的暖風，寶貝
告訴我你是我永遠的朋友，寶貝
我們的情誼直到永遠，寶貝
再一次，寶貝，我要說
我渴望自由

（洪靚 譯）

精彩之處

Don't try me： 在這裏的意思是如果你的愛會束縛我，那麼不要嘗試去愛我，因為我要的是自由。

這首歌悠然、抒情，歌詞浪漫，如一首情詩，充滿愛情的美好憧憬。歌詞中有大量押韻的使用，如 free、be 和 sea，hand 和 sand，sun 和 fun，thing 和 string 等，不但發音豐富和諧，悅耳動聽，也為聽者帶來一幅幅愛情的美好畫面。

Mr. Big

▶ NOW PLAYING

To Be with You
與你同在

英文
歌詞

Hold on little girl
Show me what he's done to you
Stand up little girl
A broken heart can't be that bad
When it's through, it's through
Fate will **twist** the both of you
So come on baby come on over
Let me be the one to show you

I'm the one who wants to be with you
Deep inside I hope you feel it too
Waited on a line of greens and blues
Just to be the next to be with you

Build up your confidence
So you can be on top for once
Wake up who cares about
Little boys that talk too much
I seen it all go down
Your game of love was all **rained out**
So come on baby come on over
Let me be the one to hold you

Why be alone when we can be together baby
You can make my life worthwhile
And I can make you start to smile

⏸ 詞彙
註釋

twist *v.* 轉變

build up 逐步建立

rain out 毀滅

此曲是大人物樂隊（Mr. Big）最為出色的流行搖滾作品之一。該隊其實是一支重金屬樂隊，但這歌別樹一格，展現樂隊粗獷以外的柔情一面，結果大受歡迎。其中主音 Eric Martin 的深情演繹以及結他手 Paul Gilbert 的結他掃弦功不可抹。這首歌也曾被西城男孩（Westlife）翻唱過。

 中文譯文

等一下，女孩
告訴我，他對你做了甚麼
堅強點，女孩
心碎並沒有想像中那麼糟糕
都已經過去了，就不要太在意了
命運將會為你開啟新的篇章
過來寶貝，請靠近我
讓我告訴你

我就是那個想和你在一起的人
我深深地期待你也能感受到
路途漫漫，我等候許久
讓我成為下一個陪伴你的人吧

重拾你的自信
度過命運的坎坷
找出那個真正懂得你的人
那些不懂你的人任由他們說吧
我看着一切平息下來
你的愛情遊戲毀滅了
過來寶貝，請靠近我
讓我抱着你

寶貝，既然我們可以在一起，為何獨自忍受孤獨
你使我的生命更有意義
我可以讓你重拾甜蜜的微笑

（任欣 譯）

 精彩之處

I'm...too：這是一個由關係代詞 who 引導的定語從句，突出強調了「我」的款款深情和濃厚情誼，期待着對方能夠體會到「我」的感情，期待着「我」就是那個陪伴的人。

I seen...rained out：此句話展示了「我」作為旁觀者目睹對方發生的一切，告誡對方上段感情已經結束，不要再糾結和痛苦。重拾信心，「我」會陪伴身旁。

歌曲最後兩句歌詞 You can make my life worthwhile 和 And I can make you start to smile，結構整齊，句尾單詞 worthwhile 和 smile 構成尾韻，讀來朗朗上口，體現音韻美與和諧美。

Norah Jones

Don't Know Why
不 知 為 何

英文 歌詞

I waited 'til I saw the sun
I don't know why I didn't come
I left you by the house of fun
I don't know why I didn't come
I don't know why I didn't come

When I saw the break of day
I wished that I could fly away
Instead of kneeling in the sand
Catching **teardrops** in my hand

My heart is drenched in wine
But you'll be on my mind forever

Out across the endless sea
I would die in **ecstasy**
But I'll be a bag of bones
Driving down the road alone

My heart is drenched in wine
But you'll be on my mind forever

Something has to make you run
I don't know why I didn't come
I feel as empty as a drum
I don't know why I didn't come
I don't know why I didn't come
I don't know why I didn't come

⏸ 詞彙 註釋

teardrop *n.* 淚滴

ecstasy *n.* 狂喜

這首歌取自 21 世紀最暢銷的美國爵士歌手諾拉·鍾斯（Norah Jones）的首張專輯《遠走高飛》（*Come Away with Me*）。這張專輯為她一舉贏得第 45 屆格林美共 8 項大獎，其中包括年度最佳唱片、最佳專輯、最佳新人、最佳流行女歌手和最佳流行專輯等 5 項個人大獎。

中文譯文

我的心在等待，直到看見日出
不知為何我沒有出現
我把你一個人留在溢滿快樂的屋子裏
不知為何我沒有出現
不知為何我沒有出現

黎明破曉時分
我多麼希望自己可以飛走
而不是跪在沙灘上
雙手捧着自己的淚珠

我用酒把自己灌醉
但你永遠留在我心裏

跨越茫茫大海
我願在狂喜中離去
但我骨瘦如柴的軀體
仍將在路上孤獨行走

我用酒把自己灌醉
但你已永遠留在我心裏

一些事情使你離開了我
我不知為何自己沒有出現
我的心空蕩如鼓
我不知為何自己沒有出現
我不知為何自己沒有出現
我不知為何自己沒有出現

（顏豔 譯）

 精彩之處

My heart is drenched in wine：指寄情於酒，用酒來麻醉自己的心。

a bag of bones：意為「骨瘦如柴的人」，此句蘊含有「衣帶漸寬終不悔，為伊消得人憔悴」的意境。

as empty as a drum：心空蕩如鼓，這裏運用了比喻的修辭手法，形象細膩地表達了失去戀人後心中的那種痛苦、失落與孤獨。

這首歌節奏舒緩，配上歌手溫柔而又略顯哀傷的嗓音，深深打動聽眾的心。這首歌歌詞也宛如一首情詩，有大量尾韻的使用，如 sun 和 fun，day 和 away，hand 和 sand，bone 和 alone，drum 和 come 等，不僅為聽眾帶來一幅幅生動的意象，同時發音朗朗上口，體現音韻美以及和諧美。

Norah Jones

New York City
紐 約

I can't remember what I planned tomorrow
I can't remember when it's time to go
When I look in the mirror
Tracing lines with a pencil
I remember what came before
I wanted to think there was endless love
Until I saw the light **dim** in your eyes
In the dead of the night I found out
Sometimes there's love that won't survive

New York City
Such a beautiful disease
New York City
Such a beautiful
Such a beautiful disease

Laura kept all her disappointments
Locked up in a box behind her closet door
She pulled the **blinds** and listened to the thunder
With no way out from the family store
We all told her things could get better
When you just say goodbye
I'll lay awake one more night
Caught in a vision I want to deny

And did I mention the note that I found
Taped to my locked front door
It talked about no regrets
As it slipped from my hand to the scuffed tile floor
I rode the train for hours on end
And watched the people pass me by
It could be that it has no end
Just an action junkie's **lullaby**

We were full of the stuff that every dream rested
As if floating on a lumpy pillow sky
Caught up in the whole illusion
That dreams never pass us by
Came to a tattooed conclusion
That the big one was knocking on the door
What started as a mass delusion
Would take me far from the place I adore

詞彙註釋

dim *adj.* 黯淡的

blind *n.* 百葉窗

lullaby *n.* 搖籃曲

這首歌是美國爵士歌手諾拉·鍾斯（Norah Jones）的經典作品之一，收錄在 2003 年的專輯《紐約》（*New York City*）中。專輯由藍調大師彼得·馬力克（Peter Malick）和諾拉·鍾斯共同製作，為諾拉·鍾斯藍調風格奠定基調。

 中文譯文

望着鏡子
我忘了明日的計劃
也忘了出發的時間
追隨着鉛筆字跡
過去的一切 歷歷在目
我曾相信 愛情恒久
直到我望見你失落的眼神
深夜時分 我終於醒悟
有時候 愛情沒有天長地久

紐約呀 紐約
你真是一場美麗的疾病
紐約呀紐約
你真美
你真是一場美麗的疾病

蘿拉將所有的失意和沮喪
鎖進盒子 藏於衣櫥
拉開百葉窗，聽着窗外雷聲轟鳴
她離不開家庭小店
我們安慰她 一切將安好
若你告別
我將徹夜難眠
一個不堪回首的畫面，縈繞腦海

對了，我還發現
緊鎖的房門上 貼着一張字條
上面寫道：無後悔之意
我啞口無言，字條滑過指尖，落在破舊的瓷磚地板
我長時間地乘着火車
我坐上賓士不停的列車
看着人來人往，永無止境
好似一首搖籃曲

我們曾滿懷希望
猶如一朵飄浮的雲彩
沉迷於幻想中
還以為夢想不再遙遠
貿然地下了定義
因為門外的敲門聲
而開始的卻是雜亂的幻想
把我從愛慕的地方帶到遠方

（王先哲　譯）

 精彩之處

Such...disease：beautiful 通常形容人美麗，和 disease 看似格格不入，但實際上該句運用了比喻的修辭手法，形容紐約為「美麗的疾病」，富有雙重含義。一方面，紐約是一座華麗的國際都市；另一面，大都市催生了諸多「都市病」。

The Story
故 事

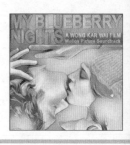

I don't know how to begin
'Cause the story has been told before
I will sing along I suppose
I guess it's just how it goes

And now those springs in the air
I don't go down anyway
I guess it's just how it goes
The stories have all been told before

But if you don't try
The light won't hit your eyes
And the moon won't rise and fall in sight

I don't know how it'll end
Though the records play
I guess it's just how it goes
The stories have all been told before
I guess it's just how it goes
The stories have all been told before

這首歌是電影《藍莓之夜》（*My Blueberry Nights*）的主題曲，該歌曲的演唱者正是電影女主角諾拉·鍾斯。諾拉在獲得 1997 年「最佳爵士歌手」音樂獎後，簽入美國著名的爵士樂加工廠藍色音符（Blue Note），成為該公司最年輕的爵士女歌手。

我不知如何開始
因為故事早已被訴説
我想我會繼續歌唱
我猜這才是它繼續的方式

現在那如噴泉般噴向空中
無論如何我不會下落
我猜這就是它繼續的方式
故事早已被訴説

但你如果不去嘗試
就不會看到希望的曙光
就不會看到月出月落

我不知故事會如何結局
故事一幕幕重演
我猜這就是它繼續的方式
故事早已被訴説
我猜這就是它繼續的方式
故事早已被訴説

（蔣夢陽 譯）

 **精彩
之處**

spring in the air：這裏採用了比喻的修辭手法，將腦海中對故事的回想比喻成如噴泉般湧現，十分形象生動。

**light won't hit your
eyes**：這首歌多次採用比喻的修辭手法，這裏光芒刺痛眼睛，光芒主要代表這是一種希望，引導女主人公從失敗感情的陰影中走出來，面對新的生活。

Oasis

Don't Look Back in Anger
莫 為 往 事 而 怒

英文
歌詞

Slip inside the eye of your mind
Don't you know you might find
A better place to play
You said that you'd never been
But all the things that you've seen
Will slowly fade away

So I start the revolution from my bed
'Cause you said the brains I have went to my head
Step outside the summertime's **in bloom**
Stand up beside the fireplace
Take that look from off your face
You ain't ever gonna burn my heart out

So Sally can wait
She knows it's too late as we're walking on by
Her soul slides away
But don't look back in anger I heard you say

Take me to the place where you go
Where nobody knows if it's night or day
Please don't put your life in the hands
Of a rock and roll band
Who'll throw it all away

⏸ 詞彙
註釋

in bloom （鮮花）盛
開

So Sally can wait
She knows it's too late as we're walking on by
My soul slides away
Don't look back in anger
I heard you say

這是英國搖滾樂隊綠洲樂隊（Oasis）成名作之一，創作於 1995 年，是一首言簡意賅卻意味深長的英倫搖滾歌曲。其曲風輕快活躍、生機勃勃、催人奮進。作為單曲發行，曾登上英國單曲排行榜冠軍寶座，並成為 1996 年十大暢銷單曲之一。

 中文譯文

腦海裏不停探索
難道你不明白
你或將發現一片全新樂土
你說你不曾到達
但你今天一切所見所聞
終將漸漸褪色

所以我從床上發起一場變革
因為你說過，我已找回理智
要走出家門，感受繁花似錦的夏日
要站在壁爐前，腰板挺直
讓臉上的陰霾，全部消失
我內心的熱情，永遠不息

薩莉願意等待
我們悄然走過，她才知為時已晚
她的靈魂不再束縛
你說道，莫為往事而怒

請帶我去你的樂土
那裏人們不舍晝夜
切勿將命運拱手相讓
為一個搖滾樂隊掌控
因為它只會揮霍生命

薩莉願意等待
我們悄然走過時，她才知為時已晚
我的靈魂不再束縛
莫為往事而怒
我聽到你在說

（王先哲 譯）

 精彩之處

歌曲是作者的自述。歌詞 beside the fireplace 與作者兒時全家在壁爐旁照相的經歷息息相關。歌曲展現了作者豁達的處世態度和對自由的嚮往。歌名 Don't Look Back in Anger 本身就是一句含義深刻的格言，鼓勵人們笑對往事，積極迎接未來。

So I start the revolution from my bed：該句是在向披頭四樂隊主唱約翰·連儂宣導的「床上和平」致敬。1969 年為號召人們反對越戰，連儂和妻子小野洋子發起了為期兩週的「床上和平運動」，旨在以靜坐等非暴力形式呼籲世界和平。

brains：brain 作複數可指「智慧，智力」。例如：He is nice, but he hasn't got much brains.（他為人很好，但並不聰明。）

Stand by Me
我 們 在 一 起

英文
歌詞

Made a meal and **threw it up** on Sunday
I've got a lot of things to learn
Said I would and I'll be leaving one day
Before my heart starts to burn

So what's the matter with you
Sing me something new don't you know
The cold and wind and rain don't know
They only seem to come and go away

Times are hard when things have got no meaning
I've found a key upon the floor
Maybe you and I will not believe in the things we
find
Behind the door

Stand by me,
nobody knows the way it's gonna be

If you're leaving will you take me with you
I'm tired of talking on my phone
There is one thing I can never give you
My heart can never be your home

⏸ 詞彙
註釋

throw up 嘔吐

stand by sb. 與某人
同在

The way it's gonna be, baby I can see
Don't you know the cold and wind and rain don't
know
They only seem to come and go away

這首歌是英國搖滾樂隊綠洲（Oais）樂隊的代表作之一，收錄於 1997 年的專輯《現在集合》（*Be Here Now*）中，曾於 1997 年 9 月榮膺英國歌曲排行榜亞軍。該歌曲為英倫搖滾曲風，由樂隊主音諾埃爾·加拉格爾（Noel GallagherIn）創作。這歌保持了綠洲樂隊富有節奏感的搖滾風格。

中文譯文

為自己做了頓飯，結果周日全吐了出來
我要學的還真不少呢
我説過，趁我未心生厭倦
我將啟程離開

你過得怎麼樣
給我講講新鮮事吧　難道你不明白
那些嚴寒和風雨
總是來來往往，千篇一律

若生活失去意義，日子將無比艱難
可我已想好出路
儘管你我
或許仍不相信
就在大門之後

請伴我同行吧
就算前路茫茫，無人看透

若你離去，可否讓我陪伴你
我已厭倦電話裏的喧囂紛擾
可是有件事我不能答應
我的心你永遠無法佔有

親愛的，我已看破紅塵
那些嚴寒和風雨
就是來來往往
千篇一律

（王先哲　譯）

精彩之處

作者作詞時遭遇一段小插曲：在母親反覆叮囑下，他決定不再外出就餐而改為親自下廚，可沒幾日便食物中毒。歌詞開篇講述的就是這段經歷。歌曲以慵懶的曲調為前奏，之後漸入佳境，恰好展現了作者從千篇一律的生活中覺醒，迫切渴望新鮮感，不願為人束縛的心境。

Times are hard： 形容世事艱難或日子不好過。

Oasis

Wonderwall
迷 牆

英文
歌詞

Today is gonna be the day that
They're gonna throw it back to you
By now you shoulda somehow
Realized what you gotta do
I don't believe that anybody
Feels the way I do about you now

Backbeat, the word is on the street
That the fire in your heart is out
I'm sure you've heard it all
Before but you never really had a doubt
I don't believe that anybody
Feels the way I do about you now

And all the roads we have to walk are **winding**
And all the lights that lead us there are **blinding**
There are many things that I would like to say to you
But I don't know how

Because maybe
You're gonna be the one that saves me
And after all
You're my wonderwall

詞彙
註釋

backbeat *n.* （音樂術語）基調強節奏（此處無實意，用於與 street 一詞形成押韻）

winding *adj.* 蜿蜒的

blinding *adj.* 令人眼花繚亂的

這首歌收錄於綠洲樂隊（Oasis）1995 年專輯《清晨的榮耀》（*Morning Glory*）中，曾在英國單曲榜排名第一，並風靡歐美樂壇，在 90 年代最佳音樂排名中也名列前茅。2012 年倫敦奧運會閉幕式該歌曲再次演繹，喚起樂迷們心中無限的回憶。

中文譯文

今天就是這樣的日子
以後必將被人舊事重提
事到如今
你也該清楚如何應對
我對你的感覺
我相信無人能比

街上謠言紛飛
說你已心灰意冷
我相信你都已聽過
但你心中從未遲疑
我對你的感覺
我相信無人能比

我們的前路蜿蜒曲折
指路的燈光炫目刺眼
對你我有
千言萬語
卻不知如何表達

或許因為
你就是我的救世主
歸根結底
你就是我的迷牆

（王先哲　譯）

精彩之處

這首歌的歌名選自 1968 年同名電影，直譯為「迷牆」，可理解為令人迷戀的事物，主音諾埃爾·加拉格爾曾承認該歌曲是為其當年未婚妻所作，但又在離婚後改口。其輕快的結他前奏，撲朔迷離的歌詞，如「謎」一樣，眾說紛紜，耐人尋味。

feel the way I do：意為「與我同感」，do 代指 feel，同時又包含短語 feel about sth.，表示「對……的感覺或看法」。

第一段連用了 gonna、shoulda、gotta 的連讀方式，一方面表現出前後照應，另一方面體現了歌曲類似獨白的特性，使歌詞口語化。

Every Breath You Take
你 的 每 一 次 呼 吸

英文
歌詞

Every breath you take
Every move you make
Every **bond** you break
Every step you take
I'll be watching you
Every single day
Every word you say
Every game you play
Every night you stay
I'll be watching you

Oh can't you see
You belong to me
How my poor heart aches
With every step you take

Every move you make
Every **vow** you break
Every smile you **fake**
Every claim you stake
I'll be watching you

Since you've gone I've been lost without a trace
I dream at night, I can only see your face
I look around but it's you I can't replace
I feel so cold and I long for your embrace
I keep crying baby, baby, please

Oh can't you see
You belong to me
How my poor heart aches
With every step you take

詞彙
註釋

bond *n.* 束縛

vow *n.* 誓言

fake *v.* 偽裝

這首歌在 1983 年的公告牌排行榜上曾蟬聯八週冠軍。歌曲在 1997 年被吹牛老爹（Puff Daddy）改編為另一首暢銷單曲《我會想念你》（I'll Be Missing You），而其原唱者警察樂隊（The Police），是 1977 年在英國倫敦成立的三人搖滾樂隊。

中文譯文

你的每次呼吸
你的每個動作
你掙脫的每個束縛
你邁出的每一步
我都將看着你
每一天
你説的每個字
你玩過的每個把戲
每個你存在的夜晚
我都將看着你

哦，難道你看不見嗎
你是屬於我的
我的心是這樣痛
你的每一步

每一個動作
每個未能遵守的諾言
每次假惺惺的笑
你的每個表白
我都將注視你

你走之後，我失去了你的消息
我只能在夜裏夢見你的容顏
我四處尋找，但是你是這樣的無可替代
我覺得渾身冰冷 極度渴望你的擁抱
我只能不住得哭泣 寶貝求求你

啊，難道你還看不出嗎
你是屬於我的
我的心是這樣得痛
你的每一步

（楊亞男　譯）

精彩之處

Every breath you take：
這首歌曲的詞作者史汀說道，一天午夜醒來，這句詞就一直縈繞在腦海中，於是便坐到鋼琴前，用了半個小時寫出了這首歌。旋律雖然很大眾化，但是歌詞卻很有趣。歌詞運用重複的手法表示對主人翁的無限思念。

I look around...replace：
我四處尋找，但是你是這樣地無可替代，這句歌詞的畫面感極強，似乎可以看見主人翁的無助和痛哭掙扎。

這首歌旋律動聽，演唱者激情澎湃，聲音具有強烈的震撼力。這首歌的歌詞很像一首優美的詩歌，韻腳整齊，錯落有致，如 take、make 和 break，day、say、play 和 stay，trace、face、replace 和 embrace 等，發音時或以爆破音 [k] 結尾，或以雙母音 [ei] 結尾，聲音和諧響亮，體現音韻美。

You Will Be in My Heart
你 一 直 都 在 我 心 裏

Come, stop your crying, it will be all right
Just take my hand, hold it tight
I will protect you from, all round you
I will be here, don't you cry
For one so small, you seem so strong
My arms will hold you
Keep you safe and warm
This **bond** between us can't be broken
I will be here, don't you cry

Because you'll be in my heart
Yes, you'll be in my heart
From this day on
Now and forever more
You'll be in my heart
No matter what they say
You'll be here in my heart, always

Why can't they understand the way we feel
They just don't trust what
They can't explain
I know we're different
But deep inside us, we're not that different at all

And you'll in my heart
Yes, you'll in my heart
From this day on,
Now and forever more

Don't listen to them
'Cause what do they know
We need each other
To have, to hold
They'll see in time

When **destiny** calls you
You must be strong
I may not be with you
But you've got to hold on
They'll see in time
We'll show them together

**詞彙
註釋**

bond *n.* 紐帶

destiny *n.* 命運

這首輕柔搖滾歌曲由英國搖滾巨星菲爾·科林斯（Phil Collins）演唱，收錄在電影原聲專輯《泰山》（*Tanzan*）中。這首歌作為迪士尼著名電影裏的經典曲目，在 1999 年獲得奧斯卡最佳電影歌曲獎和金球獎最佳電影歌曲獎。

中文譯文

不要哭，一切都會好
拉住並握緊我的手
不要哭，我將陪伴你
一直陪伴在你左右
你個子雖小卻很堅強
我會緊緊擁抱着你
帶給你安全和溫暖
我們的紐帶不會斷
不要哭我將陪着你

因我心中掛念着你
是的，你在我心裏
就從此時此刻開始
現在和永遠的永遠
你永遠都在我心裏
不管人們説些甚麼
你一直都在我心裏

為何他們不懂我們
他們只是無法相信
他們無法解釋的事
我知道我們不一樣
但其實沒甚麼不同

你一直都在我心裏
對，一直在我心裏
就從此時此刻開始
現在和永遠永遠

不要聽他們的言語
原因是他們知道嗎
我們要彼此在一起
一起去擁有和維持
將來他們終將明白

當命運向你召喚時
你要學會更加堅強
最後也許未在一起
但是你一定要堅持
將來他們終將明白
我們要攜手來證明

（戴衛平 譯）

精彩之處

When destiny...strong：
這兩句歌詞是作者對戀人的聲聲叮囑和勸慰。當命運向你召喚時，你必須要選擇堅強。我也許不在你身邊，但你也要勇敢地走下去。生活中的坎坷不計其數，我們既然無法選擇命運，就選擇更加堅強。

Queen

Love of My Life
我 一 生 中 的 愛

 英文
歌詞

Love of my life
You've hurt me
You've broken my heart
And now you leave me
Love of my life
Can't you see
Bring it back, bring it back
Don't take it away from me
Because you don't know
What it means to me

Love of my life
Don't leave me
You've taken my love
You now **desert** me
Love of my life
Can't you see
Bring it back, bring it back
Don't take it away from me
Because you don't know
What it means to me

You will remember
When this is **blown over**
And everything's all by the way
When I grow older
I will be there at your side to remind you
How I still love you

Back, hurry back
Please bring it back home to me
Because you don't know
What it means to me
Love of my life
Love of my life

II 詞彙
註釋

desert *v.* 遺棄

blow over 消散

這首歌曲來自英國的皇后樂隊（Queen），收錄在他們的專輯《歌劇院之夜》（*A Night at the Opera*）中。皇后樂隊完美地將華麗搖滾、前衛搖滾、古典音樂融為一體。他們的音樂影響深遠，20 多年來在世界各地的搖滾樂隊身上都能找到他們的影子。這首歌曲是他們為數不多的抒情慢歌。歌詞中交織着心碎和期冀，旋律間滲透着古典的奢華。

 中文譯文

我一生中的愛
你已深深傷害我
讓我心碎憔悴後
現在又要離開我
我一生中的愛
難道你還不明白
把我的愛帶回來
別把我的愛帶走
因為你不曾瞭解
你對於我的意義

我一生中的愛
不要轉身離開我
擁有我全部的愛
現在卻要丟下我
我一生中的愛
你真的還不明白
把我的愛帶回來
別把我的愛帶走
因為你不曾瞭解
你對於我的意義

某天你將會記得
若愛已隨風逝去
世界也黯然失色
即使到人老珠黃
還在你耳畔輕訴
我依然如此愛你

趕快回到我身邊
請將愛帶回給我
因為你不會知道
你對於我的意義
我一生中的愛
我一生中的愛

（李穎 譯）

 精彩之處

You now desert me： 此句歌詞的 desert 和上文的 leave 都表示「拋棄、丟下」的意思，作者的愛人和自己分手，離開了自己。

When this...way： 這句歌詞大意是若我們的愛隨風飄散，那麼所有的一切都會隨之飄散。你就是我的世界，若你離去，一切又將有甚麼意義？法國 19 世紀著名作家司湯達（Stendhal）曾說過：「愛就是寧可在你身邊當個奴隸，也不願離開你而去當個國王。」

What it means to me： 這句歌詞在歌中反覆吟唱，突出了歌曲的主題。means 為句中重讀單詞，語氣加強，發音飽滿拉長，具有爆發力，我們彷彿感到主人翁對愛情的那份執着，和對愛人深深的眷戀。

I Believe I Can Fly
我 相 信 我 能 飛

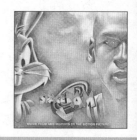

I used to think that I could not go on
And life was nothing but an awful song
But now I know the meaning of true love
I'm leaning on the **everlasting** arms

If I can see it, then I can do it
If I just believe it, there's nothing to it

I believe I can fly
I believe I can touch the sky
I think about it every night and day
Spread my wings and fly away
I believe I can **soar**
I see me running through that open door
I believe I can fly

See I was on the **verge** of breaking down
Sometimes silence can seem so loud
There are **miracles** in life I must achieve
But first I know it starts inside of me oh

Hey 'cause I believe in me
If I can see it, then I can do it
If I just believe it, there's nothing to it

詞彙
註釋

everlasting *adj.* 永遠
的

soar *v.* 翱翔

verge *n.* 邊緣

miracle *n.* 奇跡

1996 年，黑人歌手 R·凱利（R. Kelly）為「飛人」米高佐敦作詞、作曲並親自在電影《太空也入樽》（Space Jam）中演唱了這首歌。自此這首歌成為他最著名的單曲之一，1997 年第 40 屆格林美頒獎中一舉獲得三項大獎。除了上述獎項外，他曾獲 14 個告示牌音樂獎、3 個騷靈列車獎以及全美音樂獎等。

 中文譯文

我曾以為我無法堅持下去
生命不過是首悲傷的歌曲
但我現在懂得了真愛的意義
我找到了可以依靠的堅強臂膀

只要有希望我就一定能成功
只要有信念我就能戰勝一切

我相信我能飛
我相信我能觸到天空
日日夜夜，我想像
展開翅膀，飛向夢想
我相信我能翱翔
我看見自己飛越那敞開的生命之門
我相信我能飛

看到了嗎？我快要崩潰
有時候沉默也可以如此振聾發聵
那是生命的奇蹟，我需竭力達成
但我知道這始於我的內心

啊，因為我自信
只要有希望我就一定能成功
只要有信念我就能戰勝一切

（張旋 譯）

 精彩之處

nothing but：這個短語意為「除了……，甚麼都不是」，即「只不過是」。「生命不過是一首悲哀的歌曲」，用比喻形容「我」認為生命處處失意，與後文中的「生命中的奇跡」形成對比。

it starts inside of me：此句的 it 是指上文中提到的「竭力達成生命的奇跡」，而要達成這種奇跡就需要「從我的內心出發」。

If...to it：這兩句歌詞鏗鏘有力，在整首歌中穿插，反覆吟詠對夢想、信念的執着追求。

Rachael Yamagata

Duet
愛情二重奏

英文歌詞

Oh lover, hold on till I come back again
For these arms are growing tired
And my tales are wearing thin
If you're patient I will surprise
When you wake up I'll have come
All the ache will settle down
And we'll go do all the things we should have done

Yes, I remember what we said as we lay down to bed
I'll be here if you would only come back home

Oh lover, I'm lost
Because the road I've chosen **beckons** me away
Oh lover, don't you **roam**
Now I'm fighting words I never thought I'd say

I remember what we said as we lay down to bed
I'll **forgive** you if you'll just come back home

Oh lover, I know
You'll be out there and be thinking just of me
And I will find you down the road
We'll return back home to where we're meant to be

 詞彙 註釋

beckon *v.* 呼喚

roam *v.* 漫遊

forgive *v.* 寬恕

這首另類搖滾歌曲由美國歌手山形瑞秋（Rachael Yamagata）演唱，收錄在她 2008 年發行的第二張專輯《殫精竭慮》（*Elephants...Teeth Sinking Into Heart*）中。這首歌曲清澈淡雅，空靈獨特，淡淡的憂傷中滲透着一股無以名狀的魔力，彷彿能無聲無息地撫平人們心底歲月遺留下來的傷痕，讓所有的淚與痛都隨風落入塵埃。

噢，親愛的，等我，等我回來
你的擁抱已越來越無力
美好的故事越來越少
你若仍耐心等候我會驚喜不已
等你醒時我將回來
所有的傷痛都會撫平
我們一起來完成曾經的夢想

那時的我們相偎相依
話語依然縈繞在耳際
只要你回家，我會一直在這裏

噢，親愛的，我已迷失自己
我曾經選擇的路喚我離去
噢，親愛的，不要再彷徨
此刻無合適的言語形容我心情

那時的我們相偎相依，話語依然縈繞在耳際
只要你回家，我就原諒你

噢，親愛的，我堅信
你的心底依舊深深地思念着我
我會沿此路找尋到你
一起回家，因為我們註定要在一起

（李穎　譯）

精彩之處

All the ache...done： 歌詞大意是過去所有的傷痛都會平息，我們也將一起完成曾經想做而沒做的事情。從這句歌詞中我們能感受到作者樂觀堅強的生活態度和信心，以及對戀人深深的愛戀之情。

Richard Marx

▶ N O W   P L A Y I N G

Right Here Waiting
此 情 可 待

英文
歌詞

Oceans apart, day after day
And I slowly go **insane**
I hear your voice on the line
But it doesn't stop the pain
If I see you next to never
How can we say forever

Wherever you go
Whatever you do
I will be right here waiting for you
Whatever it takes
Or how my heart breaks
I will be right here waiting for you

I took for granted all the times
That I thought would last somehow
I hear the laughter
I taste the tears
But I can't get near you now

Oh, can't you see it, baby
You've got me going crazy

Wherever you go
Whatever you do
I will be right here waiting for you
Whatever it takes
Or how my heart breaks
I will be right here waiting for you

I wonder how we can survive this **romance**
But in the end if I'm with you
I'll take the chance

🄊 詞彙
註釋

insane *n.* 瘋狂

romance *n.* 愛情

李察·馬克斯（Richard Marx）是一個集作曲、填詞、演唱和音樂製作於一身的搖滾才子，1988 和 1989 年曾兩度奪得格林美「最佳搖滾男聲演唱」大獎。這首家喻戶曉的輕柔搖滾情歌就是其創作的名曲。這首歌不僅是他本人愛情的見證，也在全球受到歡迎，許多歌星演繹過不同版本。

遠隔重洋，日復一日
我一步步開始變得瘋狂
電話裏我聽到你的聲音
但這也抑制不了思念你的痛苦
倘若此生永不相見
那又何談長相廝守

不管你去哪
不管你做甚麼
我將會一直在這等你
不管命運怎樣變遷
不管我多麼心碎
我將會一直在這等你

我一直堅信
我們會堅持到最後
我聽到嘲笑聲
也嘗到淚水
可我此時不能接近你

噢，寶貝你看不到嗎
你讓我陷入癡狂

不管你去哪
不管你做甚麼
我將會一直在這等你
不管命運怎樣變遷
不管我多麼心碎
我將會一直在這等你

該如何拯救這段愛情呢
但只要最終和你在一起
我會奮不顧身

（張楠 譯）

 精彩之處

Oceans apart, day after day：oceans apart 和 day after day 分別講述作者和戀人之間地域上的距離之遠和分別時日之長。oceans apart 更是使用了比喻的手法，把距離比作遠隔重洋，形象地表達出作者與戀人的相思之苦。

Wherever you...do：句中使用 wherever 和 whatever 兩個詞，語氣深沉，不論戀人去哪、做甚麼都癡癡等待的心態表露無遺。

The Righteous Brothers

Unchained Melody
鎖不住的旋律

英文
歌詞

Oh, my love, my darling
I've **hungered for** your touch
Alone, lonely time
And time goes by so slowly
Yet time can do so much
Are you still mine
I need your love
I need your love
God, speed your love to me

Lonely rivers flow
To the sea to the sea
To the open arms of the sea
Lonely river **sigh**, wait for me
Wait for me
I'll be coming home
Wait for me

詞彙
註釋

hunger for 渴盼

sigh *v.* 歎氣

這是一首家喻戶曉的情歌，堪稱 20 世紀流行樂壇不朽之作。歌曲最初由美國組合正義兄弟（The Righteous Brothers）於 60 年代演唱，但真正讓它風靡全球的是 90 年代經典電影《人鬼情未了》（*Ghost*）。作為影片插曲，一響起就能勾起聽眾對電影的深刻回憶。隨着纏綿悠揚的旋律和富有磁性的歌聲，男女主角跨越陰陽，感天動地的愛情故事歷歷在目。

哦，我的愛，我的愛人
你的愛撫，我是多麼的渴望
在我最孤獨的時光
光陰緩緩
紛繁世界，變化萬千
你仍否在我身邊
我是如此
如此需要你的愛
願主把它帶來

淌入長河
匯入海洋
那敞開的臂膀
寂寞之河，輕輕地歎
請你等待
我將還鄉
請你等待

（王先哲　譯）

**精彩
之處**

歌名 Unchained Melody 可譯成「鎖不住的愛」或「奔放的旋律」。歌曲中流露濃濃愛意，暖人心扉，令人沉醉。

Are you still mine：該句重音落在句尾單詞 mine 上，mine 的發音飽滿、拉長並迴旋，瞬間的爆發力給聽者帶來強烈的震撼，引起共鳴，彷彿感受到主人翁濃濃的愛意和無盡的思念。

God，speed your love to me：本句中 speed 作動詞，表示「促進或加快……的速度」，用在本句中生動形象地表達了作者對愛情望眼欲穿的情懷。

歌詞後一部分描述了河流對投向大海懷抱的嚮往，實際上在借景江海之意境，表達愛人之間雖分隔兩地卻相見迫切的情感，與影片《人鬼情未了》男女主人翁之間深深的思念不謀而合，引人共鳴。

Rihanna

Diamonds
如鑽人生

Shine bright like a diamond
Find light in the beautiful sea
I chose to be happy
You and I, you and I
We're like diamonds in the sky

You're a **shooting star** I see
A vision of **ecstasy**
When you hold me, I'm alive
We're like diamonds in the sky

I knew that we'd become one right away, oh, right away
At first sight I felt the energy of sun rays
I saw the life inside your eyes

So shine bright, tonight, you and I
We're beautiful like diamonds in the sky
Eye to eye, so alive
We're beautiful like diamonds in the sky

Shine bright like a diamond
We're beautiful like diamonds in the sky

Palms rise to the universe
As we, moonshine and Molly
Feel the warmth we'll never die

⏸ 詞彙
註釋

shooting star 流星

ecstasy *n.* 狂喜，幸福

palm *n.* 棕櫚樹

◀ 188　都是愛情惹的英文歌

此曲為美國天后蕾哈娜（Rihanna）第七張專輯《毫無悔意》（Unapologetic）的首支單曲。蕾哈娜一改往日風格，少了 DJ 舞曲的驕縱，深沉而又滄桑地唱着這首為已故祖母創作的歌曲。歌曲中，現實與往昔交纏錯綜，祖母的愛與她的思念時時交織，祖母如同璀璨的鑽石、閃爍的陽光、柔和的月光。

 中文譯文

鑽石閃爍，璀璨奪目
尋遍汪洋中的光亮
我最終選擇了快樂
只有你和我，只有你和我
我們如同星空中的鑽石

你劃過夜空化為隕石
眼前再現幸福畫面
我在你懷中，開心而又眷戀
我們如同星空中的鑽石

我知道我們馬上會融為一體
馬上
初見鑽石之光，如同太陽光輝，無盡散射
閱盡了你眼中的流年

今晚，讓我隨你一起閃爍無眠
我們亦如星空中的鑽石，美麗奪目
心心相印，永無止路
我們亦如星空中的鑽石，美麗奪目

鑽石閃爍，璀璨奪目
我們亦如星空中的鑽石，美麗奪目

棕櫚樹逆勢向上
我們就來享受溫馨月光，碧海幽浪
盡享這溫暖，我們永遠不會被遺忘

（李娟 譯）

 精彩之處

At first sight... rays： 此句把鑽石之光、流星之光、太陽之光有機聯繫在一起。

I saw... eyes： 其字面意思指我看到了你眼中的生命歷程，為使句子更具美態且與下文押韻，將其譯為「閱盡了你眼中的流年」。

Molly： 為傳說中的海之女，此處用來指代大海，既包含了深厚的文化底蘊，又與前面 moonshine 押韻。

Robbie Williams

▶ N O W   P L A Y I N G

Better Man
做更好的自己

Send someone to love me
I need to rest in arms
Keep me safe from harm
In pouring rain
Give me endless summer
Lord I fear the cold
Feel I'm getting old
Before my time

As my soul heals the **shame**
I will grow through this pain
Lord I'm doing all I can
To be a better man

Go easy on my **conscience**
'Cause it's not my fault
I know I've been taught
To take the blame
Rest assured my angels will catch my tears
Walk me out of here
I'm in pain

As my soul heals the shame
I will grow through this pain
Lord I'm doing all I can
To be a better man

Once you've found that lover
You're homeward bound
Love is all around
I know some have fallen
On stony ground
But love is all around

詞彙
註釋

shame *n.* 羞愧

conscience *n.* 良心

羅比·威廉斯（Robbie Williams）是英國著名歌手，他的專輯迄今為止在全球銷量超過 5500 萬張。2002 年，羅比與 EMI 唱片公司簽下了 8000 萬英鎊的唱片合約，一舉成為英國音樂史上最有價值的歌手。

找一個人來愛我
我需要倚靠的臂彎
讓我遠離傷害
在大雨傾盆時
賜我無盡的夏日
上帝，我懼怕寒冷
我感到自己正在老去
雖正值年少

當靈魂洗脫羞愧
痛苦會教我成長
上帝，我竭盡全力
做更好的自己

別再讓我的良心受到譴責
這不是我的錯
雖然別人告訴我
該承擔過錯
相信天使會拭去我的眼淚
帶我離開這裏
我在痛苦中煎熬

當靈魂洗脫羞愧
痛苦會教我成長
上帝，我竭盡全力
做更好的自己

一旦你找到愛人
就找到了歸家的方向
愛就在身邊
我知道有人跌倒在
荒涼的土地
但愛就在身邊

（宋思怡　譯）

精彩之處

Lord I fear the cold： 這是「我」與上帝的對話，「我」的心中充滿恐懼與無助，卻無法向人述說，但又無法忍受這樣的折磨，掙扎之下，只有求助於上帝，向上帝吐露自己的心聲。

my time：指「我」現在的時光，依然年輕的時光，而「我」卻感到自己正在變老，生命之花還未綻放便已枯萎。

rest assured：是「相信、堅信」的意思，即相信上帝沒有拋棄「我」，天使會拭去「我」的眼淚。

No Ordinary Love
無 果 的 愛

I gave you all the love I got
I gave you more than I could give
I gave you love
I gave you all that I have inside
And you took my love

Didn't tell you what I believe
Did somebody say that
A love like that won't last
Didn't I give you
All that I've got to give baby

I gave you all the love I got
I gave you more than I could give
I gave you love
I gave you all that I have inside
And you took my love
You took my love

I keep crying
I keep trying for you
There's nothing like you and I baby

This is no ordinary love
No ordinary love
This is no ordinary love
No ordinary love

When you came my way
You brightened every day
With your sweet smile

這首歌選自薩德（Sade）第 4 張專輯《華麗愛情》（*Love Deluxe*），同時也是這張專輯中最受歡迎的單曲。這首歌與 1988 年的《天堂》（*Paradise*）和 1985 年的《調情聖手》（*Smooth Operator*）一起被視作薩德的經典之作。

中文譯文

給你我所有的愛
甚至透支了我的所有
給你我的愛
給你我內心深處的一切
你卻帶走了我的愛

我不曾告訴你我所想所念
有人說
這樣的愛不會長久
不想給你卻不得不給
我能夠支付的所有

給你我所有的愛
甚至透支了我的所有
給你我的愛
給你我內心深處的一切
但你卻帶走了我的愛
你帶走了我的愛

我不停地哭泣
為了你我不斷地努力
寶貝，沒有人像我們這樣戀愛

這愛與眾不同
與眾不同
這愛刻骨銘心
刻骨銘心

當你走過我身旁
世界都因你而明亮起來
帶着你甜甜的笑

（楊亞男 譯）

精彩之處

這首歌講述結婚當天新郎落跑，新娘穿着婚紗在大街上遊蕩，這解釋了 no ordinary love 的第二層意思，即「無果的愛」。但不管是哪一種都是沒有結果的，所以這首歌的主題是無果的、痛哭的愛。

歌中有多處押韻，如 give、love 和 believe，got、last 和 that，way 和 day 等，發音豐富和諧，悅耳動聽。

Savage Garden

Truly Madly Deeply
癡 迷

英文
歌詞

I'll be your dream, I'll be your wish,
I'll be your **fantasy**
I' be your hope, I'll be your love,
be everything that you need
I love you more with every breath
truly madly deeply do

I will be strong, I will be faithful
'Cause I'm counting on a new beginning
A reason for living
A deeper meaning

I wanna stand with you on a mountain
I wanna bathe with you in the sea
I wanna lay like this forever
Until the sky falls down on me

And when the stars are shining brightly in the
velvet sky
I'll make a wish send it to heaven
Then make you want to cry the tears of joy
For all the pleasure and the certainty
That we're surrounded by the comfort
And protection of the highest power
In lonely hours
The tears **devour** you

Oh can't you see it baby
You don't have to close your eyes
'Cause it's standing right before you
All that you need will surely come

⏸ 詞彙
註釋

fantasy *n.* 幻想

velvet *adj.* 天鵝絨似
的

devour *v.* 完全佔有

此曲以其優美的旋律，在美國公告牌排行榜位列第一，後來這首歌曲在 1998 年的世界榜上排名第二。1998 年 4 月，這歌更是連續 5 週成為公告牌排行榜 Hot 100 中點播率最高的歌曲，並統治了公告牌排行榜成人音樂榜達 11 週之久。

 中文譯文

我將成為你的夢想，你的願望
你的幻想
我將成為你的希望，你的愛人
你的一切的一切
伴隨着每次呼吸
我都更加癡迷於你

我會變強大，我會忠誠於你
因為我想要一個全新的開始
一個活下去的理由
一個更有意義的理由

我想要與你一同站在山頂
我想要與你一同投入大海的懷抱
我想永遠這樣躺着
直到地老天荒

當星星
在天鵝絨般的天空閃爍時
我將向上天許一個願望
美好到讓你落淚
只為這真真切切的喜悅
我們被幸福包圍
為上天庇護
孤獨歲月裏
這些美好回憶將完全佔有你

寶貝，難道你還看不出嗎
你不用閉上雙眼
這一切就擺在你面前
所有你想要的都必將來到

（楊亞男 譯）

 精彩之處

Until the sky falls down on me： 這句的意思類似中文的「山無棱，天地合」，強調愛情的強大與不可磨滅的力量。

tears devour you： 這並不是指女主人翁孤獨時會傷心落淚，聯繫前文，tears 指的是那些幸福的時光。

Scott McKenzie

San Francisco
三 藩 市 之 歌

英文
歌詞

If you're going to San Francisco
Be sure to wear some flowers in your hair
If you're going to San Francisco
You're gonna meet some gentle people there

For those who come to San Francisco
Summertime will be a loving there
In the streets of San Francisco
Gentle people with flowers in their hair

All across the nation such a strange vibration
People in motion
There's a whole generation with the new
explanation
People in motion people in motion

For those who come to San Francisco
Be sure to wear some flowers in your hair
If you come to San Francisco
Summertime will be a loving there

這首歌來自美國民歌歌手史葛·麥肯奇（Scott McKenzie）的專輯《史葛·麥肯奇之聲》（*Voice of Scott McKenzie*）。這首歌曾是電影《阿甘正傳》中的插曲，獲第 67 屆奧斯卡電影金曲獎。他的聲音懶洋洋，卻透露出一份純潔和感動。

 中文譯文

如果你要去三藩市
一定要記得頭戴鮮花
如果你要去三藩市
在那裏你將會遇見溫柔善良的人們

來三藩市的朋友們
你將在這裏度過美好的夏日時光
在三藩市的大街小巷
善良的人們頭戴鮮花

全國上下正發生着奇妙變化
人們在行動
這是詮釋愛與和平的
新一代
人們在行動，在變化

來三藩市的朋友們
一定要記得頭戴鮮花
如果你要來三藩市
你將在這裏度過一段美好的夏日時光

（顏艷　譯）

 精彩之處

上世紀 60 年代美國三藩市是嬉皮士們心中的聖地，他們崇尚自由，反對戰爭，標榜愛與和平，並以花卉作為愛與和平的象徵。這首歌描述的景象正是當時嬉皮運動的真實寫照，在髮際配上花朵是對和平的禮贊，他們常常以「花顛派」或「花童」自居。

Summertime will be... there： 在本曲中，此處的 loving 作名詞。summertime will be a loving there =summertime will be a wonderful time in San Francisco，三藩市的夏日會是個很棒的時節。

gentle： 不僅指個性溫和，也指人們愛好和平及反戰的立場。

vibration： 指震動，但在本句中是指全國彌漫着一種迥然不同的氣氛。

歌詞中 hair 和 there 押韻，vibration、motion 和 explanation 也構成尾韻，發音和諧悅耳，讀來朗朗上口。

Shakin Stevens

Because I Love You
因 為 愛 你

If I got down on my knees
And I **pleaded with** you
If I crossed a million oceans
Just to be with you
Would you ever let me down ?

If I climbed the highest mountain
Just to **hold you tight**
If I said that I would love you
Every single night
Would you ever let me down ?

Well I'm sorry if it sounds kind of sad it's just that
Worried so worried
That you let me down

Because I love you, love you
Love you so don't let me down

If I swam the longest river
Just to call your name
If I said the way I feel for you
Would never change
Would you ever fool around

Well I'm sorry if it sounds kind of bad it's just that
Worried that so worried
That you let me down
Because I love you, love you

**詞彙
註釋**

plead with 懇求

hold tight 抱緊

這是享譽「英國新貓王」之稱的希金斯·史蒂文斯（Shakin Stevens）最廣為人知的一首歌。此曲於 1986 年一炮走紅。

中文譯文

如果我跪地求你
祈求與你同在
如果我千里追尋
只求生死相隨
你會不會接受我？

如果我登頂極峰
只求與你緊緊相擁
如果我說我會愛你
一生一世
你會不會接受我？

愧疚我無法歡悅言間
只因憂心彷徨
怕你再次拒絕

因為我愛你，愛你
愛你至深，才不願孤度餘生

如果我游渡長河
呼喚你的名字
如果愛你的初心
至死不渝
你會不會接受我

抱歉我無法歡悅言間
只因憂心彷徨
怕你再次拒絕
愛你至深

（趙瑋 譯）

精彩之處

a million oceans： 英語中的 a million 或者 a thousand 等數詞加具體名詞的表達，一般都作「無盡，極多」之解。而且在很多情況下，具體意象需要抽象化延伸或擴大，如本句的 ocean 就不再為海洋之意，而指「路途，行跡」。

let sb. down： 指「令某人失望」，在此曲中即「拒絕示愛，令對方失魂落魄」之意。此處沒用 disappointed 是因為本詞更偏重於客觀的人和事產生的消極影響使主觀心理略帶不滿與挫敗感，而 down 常用於描述人物在遭受挫敗之後，心情的抑鬱與失落，傷心程度更甚於 disappointed，且更符合情歌意境。

fool around： 涵義豐富，在不同語境下可作多種解釋，也帶有「愚弄他人，虛度光陰」之意，而在此句中即「不願專情以待，坦誠接受」，實則都可以歸為「拒絕」之意，是與上段中的 let down 相照應、避免重複的同意表述。

Simon & Garfunkel

Scarborough Fair
斯 卡 伯 勒 集 市

英文
歌詞

Are you going to Scarborough Fair
Parsley, sage, rosemary and thyme
Remember me to one who lives there
She once was a true love of mine

Tell her to make me a **cambric** shirt
　(On the side of a hill in the deep forest green)
Parsley, sage, rosemary and thyme
　(Tracing of sparrow on the snow-crested ground)
Without no seams nor needle work
　(Blankets and bedclothes the child of the mountain)
Then she'll be a true love of mine
　(Sleeps unaware of the **clarion** call)

Tell her to find me an acre of land
　(On the side of a hill a sprinkling of leaves)
Parsley, sage, rosemary and thyme
　(Washed is the ground with so many tears)
Between the salt water and the sea strands
　(A soldier cleans and polishes a gun)
Then she'll be a true love of mine

词汇
註釋

cambric *n.* 細麻紗

clarion *n.* 號角

bellow *v.* 咆哮

heather *n.* 石楠屬植物

Tell her to reap it with a sickle of leather
　(War **bellows**, blazing in scarlet battalions)
Parsley, sage, rosemary and thyme
　(Generals order their soldiers to kill)
And gather it all in a bunch of **heather**
　(And to fight for a cause they've long ago forgotten)
Then she'll be a true love of mine

這是 20 世紀最著名、最成功的民歌之一。當中由保羅·西蒙（Paul Simon）和阿特·加芬克爾（Art Garfunkel）所唱的版本，收錄於他們的專輯《芫荽，鼠尾草，迷迭香和百里香》（*Parsley, Sage, Rosemary and Thyme*）中。

中文譯文

你要去斯鎮市集嗎
芫荽、鼠尾草、迷迭香和百里香
代我問候那兒的一位姑娘
她曾是我的摯愛

讓她為我做件麻衣
（綠林深處小山旁）
芫荽、鼠尾草、迷迭香和百里香
（雪地上追尋麻雀的蹤跡）
不無接縫和針腳
（山之子的毯子和被子）
她會是我的摯愛
（睡夢中不覺號角聲）

讓她為我找一畝地
（幾片葉子小山旁）
芫荽、鼠尾草、迷迭香和百里香
（淚水沖刷着大地）
在海水和海灘間
（士兵擦拭着手中的槍）
她會是我的摯愛

讓她用皮制的鐮刀收割
（戰火轟鳴，戰爭在血腥的軍隊裏爆發）
芫荽、鼠尾草、迷迭香和百里香
（將軍下達衝殺的命令）
用石楠紮成捆
（早已不知為何而戰）
她會是我的摯愛

（喬楠 譯）

精彩之處

Scarborough Fair：Scarborough 是英格蘭東北部一自治鎮的名字，音譯過來是「斯卡波羅」，因此 Scarborough Fair 可翻譯成「斯卡波羅市集」。

Parsley, sage, rosemary and thyme：四種植物的名字，一說其分別代表愛情的甜蜜、力量、忠誠和勇氣，一說其隱含「死亡」之意，暗示着遠在天涯的愛人已經逝去。這四種香草或暗指死亡的厄運，或被用作避邪物。

Remember me to：這一短語是「帶我向……問好」之意。

Simon & Garfunkel

The Sound of Silence
寂 靜 的 聲 音

英文歌詞

Hello darkness, my old friend
I've come to talk with you again
Because a vision softly **creeping**
Left its seeds while I was sleeping
And the vision that was planted in my brain
Still remains
Within the sound of silence

In restless dreams I walked alone
Narrow streets of **cobblestone**
'Neath the halo of a street lamp
I turned my collar to the cold and damp
When my eyes were stabbed by the flash of a neon light
That split the night
And touched the sound of silence

And in the **naked light** I saw
Ten thousand people, maybe more
People talking without speaking
People hearing without listening
People writing songs that voices never share
And no one dare
Disturb the sound of silence

Fools said I, you do not know
Silence like a cancer grows
Hear my words that I might teach you
Take my arms that I might reach you
But my words like silent raindrops fell
And echoed in the wells of silence

And the people bowed and prayed
To the neon god they made
And the sign flashed out its warning
In the words that it was forming
And the sign said, the words of the prophets
Are written on the subway walls
And tenement halls
And whispered in the sounds of silence

Ⅱ 詞彙註釋

creep *v.* 蔓延

cobblestone *n.* 鵝卵石

naked light 明火

這首歌創作於 1964 年，由民歌二人組西蒙（Simon）和加芬克爾（Garfunkel）演唱。1965 年 9 月作為單曲發行後，備受好評。1967 年作為美國電影《畢業生》（*The Graduate*）的主題曲更是為廣大聽眾所熟知。

你好啊，黑夜，我的老朋友
我又來找你聊天了
因為在我熟睡的時候
一幅畫面悄悄潛入 留下許多種子
根植在我的腦海裏
揮之不去
伴隨着寂靜的聲音

我獨自徜徉在無邊的夢境
走在狹窄的鵝卵石小道上
頭頂着街燈的光暈
我翻理着衣領抵擋嚴寒和潮濕
霓虹燈的光芒射入我的眼睛
劈開了黑暗
打破了沉寂

就在這明亮的光芒中
我看到了無數的身影
他們的交流空洞蒼白
他們的傾聽漫不經心
他們歌曲無法引起共鳴
然而沒有人敢去
破壞這份沉寂

我衝他們喊道：愚蠢的人啊
難道你們不知道，沉寂會像腫瘤一樣生長
請聽進我的話，我才能啟發你
請抓住我的手，我才能挽救你
可是我的話語就像無聲的雨滴
落入了沉寂的深井

人們躬身祈禱
膜拜他們創造的霓虹燈神
燈神散發警告的光芒
光芒逐漸變成文字
字字顯示先知的話語
早已刻在地鐵的牆上
早已刻在出租屋的門廊
人們也早已將它輕聲傳誦

（王晶 譯）

精彩之處

People...share：這首歌描述的是作者夢中的幻影，其實是對現實的抨擊，作者抨擊人們談話空洞，言之無物；聽話的人左耳聽右耳出，心不在焉；寫歌來唱卻唱得言不由衷，毫無情感。

Skeeter Davis

The End of the World
世 界 末 日

英文
歌詞

Why does the sun go on shining
Why does the sea rush to shore
Don't they know it's the end of the world
'Cause you don't love me anymore

Why do the birds go on singing
Why do the starts glow above
Don't they know it's the end of the world
It ended when I lost your love

I wake up in the morning and I wonder
Why everything is the same as it was
I can't understand, no, I can't understand
How life goes on the way it does

Why does my heart go on beating
Why do these eyes of mine crying
Don't they know it's the end of the world
It ended when you said goodbye

這首歌是美國鄉村音樂女歌手史琪特·大衛絲（Skeeter Davis）最著名的金曲。史琪特·大衛絲是美國著名的女鄉村音樂歌手，一生共獲得過 5 次格林美鄉村最佳女歌手大獎提名，並先後 4 次榮獲該獎項。2009 年的電影《美國情事》（*An American Affair*）選擇這歌作為片尾曲，傳達出了直抵人心的傷感。

中文譯文

為何陽光依然閃耀
海浪仍舊沖刷着海岸
難道不覺世界已坍塌
只因你已不再愛我

為何鳥兒依然歌唱
星星仍舊在夜空閃爍
難道不覺末日來臨
當我失去你的愛時，世界就已坍塌

清晨醒來，我仍困惑
為何一切依然如故
我不明白，是的！我真的不明白
生活如何一如往昔

為何我的心依然跳動
淚水仍舊盈滿了眼眶
末日來臨就在今朝
當你說出再見，一切都已完結

（宋思怡 譯）

精彩之處

It ended...love： it 指 代 my world，意思是失去了你的愛，雖然地球依然轉動，陽光依然耀眼，海水如往昔一般潮漲潮落，而我的世界卻早已分崩離析，不復往日的光澤，對我而言，末日已經到來。

Why everything...was： 意思是「為何一切依然如故」，「一切」指的是前文中提到的陽光、海浪、星星、鳥兒，它們沒有因「我」的哀愁而傷感，還是一如往常般歡樂。明快的氛圍恰好與「我」的悲傷形成對比，流露出少女無處訴說的憂傷。

歌曲中多處出現了以 why 開頭而以 [iŋ] 為尾韻的問句， 如 why...shinging、 why...singing、 why...beating 和 why...crying，既賦予歌詞深刻的哲理，同時加強語氣使歌曲節奏分明，體現出音韻美。

Mama
媽 媽

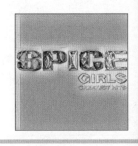

 英文歌詞

She used to be my only enemy and never let me be free
Catching me in places that I knew I shouldn't be
Every other day I **crossed the line** I didn't mean to be so bad
I never thought you would become the friend I never had

Back then I didn't know why
Why you were **misunderstood**
So now I see through your eyes
All that you did was love

Mama I love you, Mama I care
Mama I love you,
Mama my friend, you're my friend

I didn't want to hear it then but I'm not **ashamed** to say it now
Every little thing you said and did was right for me
I had a lot of time to think about, about the way I used to be
Never had a sense of my responsibility

But now I'm sure I know why
Why you were misunderstood
So now I see through your eyes
All I can give you is love

詞彙 註釋

cross the line 犯錯

misunderstand *v.* 誤解

ashamed *adj.* 慚愧的

辣妹組合（Spice Girls）是一支 90 年代極具影響力的組合，其歌曲艷俗卻有意義。這歌選自專輯《精選》（*Greatest Hits*），其銷售居英國銷量榜亞軍，並在組合的巡迴演出中得以傳播。這首歌也成為很多人成長的寫照。

 中文譯文

我曾把你當做敵人
因為你從不給我自由
你總建我回家，因為一些地方我不能停留
我時常越界犯錯
但卻不是我本意
從未想過你會成為
我前所未有的朋友

回想過去，我依然不解
當時為何會把你誤解
現在，我注視你的雙眼
發現其中真愛滿滿

媽媽，我愛你，媽媽，我在意你
媽媽，我愛你
媽媽，你是我知己

曾經厭煩你嘮叨
如今已改變
你的一言一行都是為了我好
我不斷回想
回想我的所為
完全沒有一點責任

現在我已了解
為何曾經把你誤解
此刻，注視你的雙眼
我要給你滿滿的真愛

（李娟 譯）

 精彩之處

She used to be my only enemy and never let me be free： 第一句以第三人稱出現，彷彿是一個女兒向聽眾講述媽媽的故事。翻譯此句時，將其處理為第二人稱，使整首歌曲都是女兒與媽媽的對話。處理之後，歌曲連貫一致，脈絡清晰，感召力增強。

歌曲旋律婉轉動聽，歌詞雖簡潔樸實，卻字字情真意切，娓娓道來女兒對母親深深的愛，不禁使人感慨萬千。歌詞還巧妙地運用了押韻技巧，如 free 和 be，bad 和 had，why 和 eyes 等，讀來朗朗上口，唱來悅耳動聽。

Shape of My Heart
我 心 之 花 色

He deals the cards as a **meditation**
And those he plays never suspect
He doesn't play for the money he wins
He doesn't play for respect

He deals the cards to find answer
The sacred **geometry** of chance
The hidden law of probable outcome
The numbers lead a dance

I know that the spades are the swords of a soldier
I know that the clubs are weapons of war
I know that diamonds mean money for this art
But that's not the shape of my heart

He may play the jack of diamonds
He may lay the queen of spades
He may **conceal** a king in his hand
While the memory of it fades

And if I told you that I loved you
You'd maybe think there's something wrong
I'm not a man of too many faces
The mask I wear is one

Those who speak know nothing
And find out to their cost
Like those who curse their luck in too many places
And those who fear a lost

**詞彙
註釋**

meditation *n.* 冥想

geometry *n.* 幾何圖
形

conceal *v.* 隱藏

這首歌是電影《這個殺手不太冷》（Leon—The Professional）的插曲，演唱者為英國著名歌星，前警察樂隊（Police）主音史汀（Sting），歌曲收錄於他 1993 年的專輯《十個傳奇》（Ten Summoner's Tale）。作為一位知名的歌手，迄今為止他共獲 9 尊格林美獎盃。

中文
譯文

他把玩紙牌當做冥想
出牌從不猶豫
漠視贏得的金錢
無視他人的尊嚴

卻在牌局中尋覓答案
那幾何圖形中神秘的偶然
那可能結局背後的規律
數字翩然起舞

「葵扇」如士兵手握的利劍
「梅花」如戰場轟鳴的槍炮
在這遊戲的藝術中，「階磚」象徵金錢
皆非我心之花色

或許他出「階磚」J
也許打出「葵扇」Q
抑或手中藏有王牌 K
而這些記憶終將褪色

如果我對你說我愛你
你也許錯愕詫異
我不是有着多面的男人
所戴的面具始終如一

滔滔不絕者一無所知
終將為此付出代價
比如在哪兒都埋怨命運不公之人
以及害怕迷失之人

（喬楠 譯）

精彩
之處

the shape of my heart：在這裏把 shape 翻譯為「花色」是因為，歌曲中以撲克牌為意象，用撲克牌中的另三種花色：葵扇（象徵武力）、梅花（象徵權力）、階磚（象徵金錢）作對比，這三種花色都非我心，只有第四種花色紅心（象徵愛）最像我的心，故沒有把 shape 譯成「形狀」。

curse their luck：直譯過來是「詛咒幸運」之意，其實是「埋怨運氣不好，抱怨命運不公」之意。

歌曲旋律婉轉動聽，配上歌手略帶沙啞的嗓音，透出一絲淡淡的憂傷。歌詞中巧妙運用了押韻技巧，如 suspect 和 respect，chance 和 dance，art 和 heart，diamonds 和 spades 等，兩兩押韻，發音豐富和諧，同時為聽眾帶來一幅幅生動的意象。

Taylor Swift

Safe and Sound
安 然 無 恙

I remember tears streaming down your face
When I said, I'll never let you go
When all those **shadows** almost killed your light
I remember you said, don't leave me here alone
But all that's dead and gone and pass tonight

Just close your eyes
The sun is going down
You'll be all right
No one can hurt you now
Come morning light
You and I'll be safe and sound

Don't you dare look out your window darling
Everything's on fire
The war outside our door keeps **raging on**
Hold on to this lullaby
Even when the music's gone

Just close your eyes
The sun is going down
You'll be all right
No one can hurt you now
Come morning light
You and I'll be safe and sound

⏸ 詞彙
註釋

shadow *n.* 陰影

rage on 繼續

泰勒·斯威夫特（Taylor Swift），一個出色的鄉村音樂女歌手，擅長結他、鋼琴和創作。她曾獲得多項美國鄉村音樂協會頒發的大獎以及格林美大獎。這歌是為電影《飢餓遊戲》（*The Hunger Games*）量身創作的主題曲。該單曲一經發行，12小時內就成為最熱門單曲前10，並在公告牌排行榜前100上榜17週。

中文譯文

我記得你的淚水滑過臉頰
當我說我們永不分開的時候
當所有的陰影幾乎擋住你的光
我記得你曾說過：別丟下我一個人
但這一切在今晚都已是過眼雲煙

閉上眼睛
太陽正落下
你會沒事的
如今沒有人能傷害你了
當晨光出現
我們都將安然無恙

親愛的你害怕看窗外吧
一切都在燃燒
門外的戰爭仍在繼續
記得我對你唱的這首搖籃曲
音樂已經停止

閉上眼睛
太陽正落下
你會沒事的
如今沒有人能傷害你了
當晨光出現
我們都將安然無恙

（張楠 譯）

精彩之處

stream down： 該短語描述淚水像溪水一樣滑落，表明了戀人之間的難捨難離，以及對戰爭將帶來的未知的恐懼心理。

killed your light： kill，為擬人手法，把戰爭恐懼以及分離痛苦的 shadows（陰影）擬人化。這句話可解讀為是這種陰霾使得生活黯然失色。

Don't you...darling： 用否定疑問的形式更加重了強調的語氣，表明了對窗外戰爭的恐懼心理。

City of Blinding Lights
炫目燈光之城

 The more you see the less you know
The less you find out as you grow
I knew much more then than I do now
Neon heart, day-glow eyes
The city lit by **fireflies**
They're advertising in the skies
And people like us

And I miss you when you're not around
I'm getting ready to leave the ground

Oh you look so beautiful tonight
In the city of blinding lights

Don't look before you laugh
Look ugly in a photograph
Flash bulbs, purple **irises** the camera can't see
I've seen you walk unafraid
I've seen you in the clothes you've made
Can you see the beauty inside of me
What happened to the beauty I had inside of me

Time, time, time
Won't leave me as I am
But time won't take the boy out of this man

詞彙
註釋

firefly *n.* 螢火蟲

iris *n.* 彩虹色

這首歌收錄於搖滾樂隊 U2 在 2004 年發行的《如何拆除定時炸彈》（*How to Dismantle an Atomic Bomb*）。2008 年奧巴馬競選美國總統期間，這首歌被選為競選歌曲之一，奧巴馬曾說這是他最喜歡的歌曲之一。同年，NASA 使用這首歌曲作為 STS-126 太空梭的早安曲。

 中文譯文

看到的越多，知道的就越少
成長的路上，你的發現越來越少
那時的我知道得比現在多很多
霓虹之心，陽光之眼
城市被螢火蟲點亮
它們在天空中閃耀
人們喜歡我們

當你不在身邊的時候，我想念你
我已經準備好飛離地面

今夜，你如此美麗
在燈光炫麗的城市之中

笑過後再看照片
裏面的你不上相
相機照不出輝煌的燈火，五彩的霓虹
我看着你無畏地走過
我看你穿着自做的衣服
你能窺到我內心的美麗嗎
那些美麗都怎麼了

時光啊時光
不會讓我永葆現在的模樣
但時光改變不了這個男子內心的童真

（陳穎 譯）

 精彩之處

the beauty inside of me：這個短語是指內心的美麗，也就是我們俗稱的內在美，同時還可以用 the inner beauty 來表達。

take the boy out of this man：這裏的 boy 和 man 並不是兩個人之間的對比，而是一個人幼年和成年的對比。所以我們可以將其理解為「褪去這個男人的純真」。

歌詞中運用了大量尾韻，如 know 和 grow，flies 和 fireflies，ground 和 around，tonight 和 light，laugh 和 graph，以及 feel 和 steal 等，讀起來富有節奏感，朗朗上口，悅耳動聽。

▶ N O W   P L A Y I N G

I Still Haven't Found What I'm Looking for
我 還 未 找 到 我 要 追 尋 的

英文
歌詞

I have climbed the highest the mountains
I have run through the fields
Only to be with you
I have run
I have **crawled**
I have **scaled** these city walls
Only to be with you

But I still haven't found what I'm looking for

I have kissed honey lips
Felt the healing in her fingertips
It burned like a fire
This burning desire
I have spoken with the tongue of angels
I have held the hand of a devil
It was warm in the night
I was cold as a stone

But I still haven't found what I'm looking for

I believe in the Kingdom Come
Then all the colors will bleed into one
But yes I'm still running

⏸ 詞彙
註釋

crawl *v.* 匍匐而行

scale *v.* 攀登

bonds *n.* 鐐銬

chains *n.* 枷鎖

You broke the **bonds**
And you loosened the **chains**
Carried the cross
Oh my shame
You know I believe it

這首歌收錄在 U2 樂隊的第五張專輯《約書亞樹》（*The Joshua Tree*）中。他們憑藉這張專輯獲得了兩項格林美大獎。U2 的創作內容十分廣泛，其中不乏敏感的政治性話題，如社會公平正義、人權問題等。主唱博諾（Bono）曾因他為改善非洲貧困狀況做出的努力而獲得過諾貝爾和平獎提名。

我攀登上了最高峰
我越過了無數田野
只為能和你在一起
我奔跑
我匍匐
我爬過這些城牆
只為能和你在一起

但我還未找到我要追尋的

我親吻過無數香唇
感受她指尖的愛撫
如烈火般燃燒
這似火的欲望
我曾和天使對話
也曾和惡魔握手
溫暖的夜晚
我冷若寒石

但我還未找到我要追尋的

我堅信王國將會建立
所有人們團結在一起
但我仍在奔跑

衝破束縛
打碎枷鎖
帶着十字架
承載着我的恥辱
我信仰它

（葛婷婷　譯）

 精彩之處

color：本身是「顏色」之意，但在這裏喻指具有不同膚色的人們。

歌 中 fingertips 和 lips，fire 和 desire，angels 和 devils 等兩兩押韻，不但發音和諧動聽，也給聽眾帶來種種豐富的意象。

With or Without You
你 若 即 若 離

**英文
歌詞**

See the stone set in your eyes

See the **thorn twist** in your side

I wait for you

Sleight of hand and twist of fate

On a bed of nails she makes me wait

And I wait without you

With or without you

Through the storm we reach the shore

You give it all but I want more

And I'm waiting for you

With or without you

I can't live

With or without you

And you give yourself away

And you give

And you give yourself away

My hands are tied

My body **bruised**

She's got me with

Nothing to win and nothing left to lose

**⏸ 詞彙
註釋**

thorn *n.* 刺

twist *v.* 扭曲

sleight of hand 花招

bruised *adj.* 青腫的

愛爾蘭最偉大的搖滾樂隊 U2 共獲得過 22 項格林美大獎，7 項全英音樂獎，14 項愛爾蘭流星音樂獎，1 項全美音樂獎等等。他們成名於上世紀 80 年代，但至今仍活躍在世界樂壇。這首歌是 U2 的經典作品之一。

中文譯文

你的眼神冷若冰霜
你拒人於千里之外
我在等待
命運註定一切
我焦急地等待
一直在等待，縱然你不在
你若即而又若離

我們經歷風雨，達到彼岸
你付出全部，而我欲求更多
我一直在等待

你若即而又若離
我在痛不欲生
你卻若即若離

你放棄了自我
你放棄了
你放棄了自我

我無能為力
我傷痕累累
她讓我變得
一無所有

（葛婷婷　譯）

精彩之處

See the stone...side：這兩個小短句綜合運用了英語中平行、比喻和尾韻三種修辭手法。句式平行，結構整齊，表達簡練，增強了語勢，突出了情感。歌詞中運用比喻的修辭方法，將石頭和荊棘的意象比喻為主人翁冷若冰霜，拒人於千里之外的感覺，形象生動，意味深長。

With or without you：這句歌詞貫穿全曲，歌手演唱時發音飽滿，底氣十足，帶有撕裂感，極具爆發力。我們彷彿感覺到主人公飽受愛情折磨，痛不欲生。

歌中巧妙運用了押韻技巧，如 eye 和 site，fate 和 wait，shore 和 more，give 和 live 等，韻律上使用尾韻，節奏和諧，音韻鏗鏘，一氣貫下。

Vanessa Williams

Colors of the Wind
風 的 色 彩

英文 歌詞

You think you own whatever land you land on
Earth is just a dead thing you can claim
But I know every rock and tree and creature
Has a life, has a spirit, has a name
You think the only people who are people
Are the people who look and think like you
But if you walk the footsteps of a stranger
You learn things you never knew

Have you ever heard the wolf cry to the blue corn moon ?
Or ask the grinning **bobcat** why he grinned ?
Can you sing with all the voices of the mountains ?
Can you paint with all the colors of the wind ?

Come run the hidden pine trails of the forest
Come taste the sun-sweet berries of the earth
Come roll in all the riches all around you
And for once never wonder what they're worth

The rainstorm and the rivers are my brothers
And the **heron** and the **otter** are my friends
And we are all connected to each other
In a circle in a hoop that never ends

How high does the **sycamore** grow
If you cut it down, then you'll never know
And you'll never hear the wolf cry to the blue corn moon
Or whether we are white or copper-skinned
We need to sing with all the voices of the mountains
We need to paint with all the colors of the wind

You can own the earth and still all you'll own is earth
Until you can paint with all the colors of the wind

**詞彙
註釋**

bobcat *n.* 北美大山貓

heron *n.* 蒼鷺

otter *n.* 水獺

sycamore *n.* 楓樹

這首歌是迪士尼動畫片《風中奇緣》（*Pocahontas*）的配樂歌曲，由雲妮莎·威廉斯演唱。歌曲很好的呼應了影片中深沉的感傷，卻有着自由新生的浪漫氣氛，獲得了第 68 屆奧斯卡最佳電影歌曲。

你自以為擁有你所駐足的每一塊土地
大地不過是無生命的事物可任你索求
但我知道每塊石頭、每棵樹、每個生物
都有生命，有靈性，有名字
你認為能夠稱之為人類的那些人
是那些外表和思考方式與你相似者
但假如你跟隨陌生人的腳步前行
你會有意想不到的收穫

你可曾聽到過清冷月光下野狼的哀嚎？
可曾詢問過山貓為何咧嘴而笑？
你能否和着群山中的聲音放歌？
你能否繪盡風的繽紛色彩？

來吧，在隱秘的林間小路上盡情奔跑
來吧，品嘗天然生長的美味甘甜漿果
看吧，環繞你周圍富饒的大自然
但請不要計算它們價值幾何

暴雨河流是我的兄弟
蒼鷺水獺是我的朋友
世間萬物皆不分你我
彼此相互相連

楓樹能長多高
你若將它砍倒便永遠無法知曉
你將永遠聽不到清冷月光下野狼的哀嚎
無論我們是白皮膚還是黃皮膚
我們都要和着群山中的聲音放歌
我們都要繪出風中的繽紛色彩

如果你能繪出風中的千般色彩
你才能真正擁有這個大地

（楊璐 陳穎 譯）

**精彩
之處**

blue corn moon：形容月光的清冷。

sun-sweet：被用來表達果實的純天然。

The Weepies

▶ N O W   P L A Y I N G

Gotta Have You
不能沒有你

英文
歌詞

Gray, quiet and tired and **mean**
Picking at a worried **seam**
I try to make you mad at me over the phone
Red eyes and fire and signs
I'm taken by a **nursery rhyme**
I want to make a ray of sunshine and never leave home

No amount of coffee
No amount of crying
No amount of whiskey
No amount of wine
No, no, no, no, no, nothing else will do
I've gotta have you

The road gets cold
There's no spring in the middle this year
I'm the new chicken **clucking** open hearts and ears
Oh, such a **prima Donna**
Sorry for myself
But green, it is also summer
And I won't be warm till I'm lying in your arms

I see it all through a telescope
guitar, suitcase, and a warm coat
Lying in the back of the blue boat
Humming a tune
I've gotta have you

**⏸ 詞彙
註釋**

mean *adj.* 卑微的

seam *n.* 裂縫

nursery rhyme 童謠

cluck *v.* 雞咯咯的叫聲

prima Donna 女主角

hum *v.* 哼唱

這首歌曲來自美國組合哭泣樂隊（The Weepies），收錄在其 2006 年 3 月發行的專輯《說，我是你》（*Say I Am You*）中。這張專輯發行時曾在 8 個國家的「iTunes 下載次數最多的民謠專輯榜」上攀升至首位。這首歌曲旋律簡潔流暢，淡淡的慵懶中夾雜着清新，美麗卻不張揚。

 中文譯文

蒼白，沉默，疲憊和卑微
獨自淺嘗記憶中的傷悲
想惹電話那頭的你着迷
流淚，發火，各種跡象
我沉醉在童謠的歌聲裏
想沐浴陽光
永遠待在家

咖啡沒用
哭泣沒用
威士忌沒用
美酒也沒用
不不，再多東西也沒用
我不能沒有你

人生之路讓人感覺陰冷
六月仍無溫暖的氣息
我仍像
懵懂無知的女孩
噢，這樣的一個女主角
我為自己感到遺憾傷神
即使是在這怡人的夏季
只在你懷中才感到溫暖

我用望遠鏡看到這一切
結他、行李箱和溫暖外套
躺在藍色船上
輕聲吟唱
我不能沒有你

（李穎 譯）

 精彩之處

Gray, quiet...signs：這四句歌詞中使用了幾個簡潔的意象表達了作者的狀態，頗有馬致遠《天淨沙·秋思》的味道。作者沉浸在回憶中時，滿目愁容。蒼白、沉默、疲憊和卑微四個簡潔有力的詞語，將那個默默坐在角落黯然神傷的女子刻畫得入木三分。

I'm...ears：英語俚語常用 chicken 表示女子，作者將自己比喻成剛出生的一隻敞開心扉到處嘰嘰喳喳的小雞，這暗示她內心仍然像個懵懂無知的少女，擔心心上人會覺得自己不適合做他的伴侶。

歌詞中 seam 和 rhyme，coat 和 boat，home 和 phone，warm 和 arm 等，兩兩押韻，發音生動和諧。

My Love
我 的 愛

An empty street
An empty house
A hole inside my heart
I'm all alone
The rooms are getting smaller

I wonder how
I wonder why
I wonder where they are
The days we had
The songs we sang together, Oh yeah

And oh my love
I'm holding on forever
Reaching for a love that seems so far

So I say a little prayer
And hope my dreams will take me there
Where the skies are blue
To see you once again, my love
Over seas from coast to coast
To find a place I love the most
Where the fields are green
To see you once again, my love

I try to read
I go to work
I'm laughing with my friends
But I can't stop to keep myself from thinking, oh no

To hold you in my arms
To promise you my love
To tell you from my heart
You are all I'm thinking of

這首2000年10月推出的單曲，是西城男孩（Westlife）第二張專輯《咫尺天涯》（*Coast to Coast*）的主打歌曲。它不但為其再添一首冠軍單曲，更讓他們打平了披頭四（The Beatles）連續奪冠單曲的記錄，成為繼辣妹組合（Spice Girls）之後獲得最多連續冠軍的流行音樂組合。

中文譯文

空曠的大街
空蕩的房子
心頭有一絲哀傷
無邊的孤寂包圍着我
感覺房間越來越狹小

我不知道這是怎麼了
我不明白這是為甚麼
我想知道它們在哪裏
那些我們曾經擁有的日子
那些我們共同歡唱的歌

哦，我的愛
我會始終堅持
追尋那遙不可及的愛情

於是我輕聲祈禱
希望夢想能把我帶到
那湛藍的天空下
在那裏能與你再次相見，我的愛
穿越大海，從此岸到達彼岸
去找尋我鍾愛的地方
那裏有翠綠的田野
在那裏能與你再次相見，我的愛

我埋頭讀書
我努力工作
我與朋友們盡情歡笑
但卻還是無法停止對你的思念

將你擁入懷中
向你許下諾言
發自內心地告訴你
我的心裏只有你

（李音 王晶 譯）

精彩之處

歌詞中出現了大量場景變換和描繪自然景色的詞，如：street、house、sky、coast、green field 等。 在這首歌的 MV 中，隨着歌曲的進展，背景畫面也在隨之變換，從機場到大街，從大街到車站，從車站又走到海邊，五個大男孩邊走邊唱！

Careless Whisper
無 心 私 語

 Time can never mend
The careless **whisper** of a good friend
To the heart and mind **ignorance** is kind
There's no comfort in the truth
Pain is all you'll find

I feel so unsure
As I take your hand and lead you to the dance floor
As the music dies
Something in your eyes
Calls to mind a silver screen
And all it's sad good bye

I'm never gonna dance again
Guilty feet have got no **rhythm**
Though it's easy to pretend
I know you're not a fool
I should have known better than to cheat a friend
And waste the chance that I've been given
So I'm never gonna dance again
The way I dance with you

Tonight the music seem so loud
I wish that we could lose this crowd
Maybe it's better this way
We hurt each other with the things we want to say
We could have been so good together
We could have lived this dance forever
But now who's gonna dance with me
Please stay

Now that you're gone
Was what I did so wrong so wrong
That you have to leave me alone

詞彙
註釋

whisper *v.* 私語

ignorance *n.* 無知

rhythm *n.* 節奏

這首歌出自這支英國樂隊第二張專輯《使其出名》（*Make It Big*）。該專輯連續 18 週進入排行榜前 10 名，獲得美國白金唱片銷量。這首歌在全球曾有 600 萬張銷量，在 20 多個國家排行榜上雄踞首位。

中文譯文

時間永遠無法彌合
好朋友的無心私語帶來的傷痛
無知對我的心靈也算仁慈
真相不能給我安慰
只能帶來傷痛

我心慌亂
我牽着你的手，走進舞池
舞曲終止
你的眼眸深深
讓我想起電影中的一幕
最終不過是一場別離

我無法再跳舞
內疚的腳步紛亂，錯了節奏
欺瞞豈是難事
可我知道你會看穿
坦白總比欺瞞朋友好得多
我不應失掉這最後的機會
所以我無法再跳舞
像你我從前那樣地跳舞

今晚的音樂太刺耳
我多想我們能逃離這喧囂的人群
或許這是最好的結局
喉頭的言語只會讓我們傷害彼此
我們本該好好相處
我們本該繼續跳完這支舞
但現在誰將與我共舞
請你留下來

你就要離開
我錯得太離譜
你只好離開，只剩我一人

精彩之處

mend：指「修復受傷的心」。

guilty feet：在此起一種移情的作用，與中文中「遠山含愁」的表達方法類似，即將人物的情緒植入物體。「內疚的腳步」意為「由於內疚導致腳步紛亂」。

I should...friend：此句省略了一些內容。上文中提到「我」不願再「欺瞞」（pretend），因此可推斷省略部分意為「坦白」，即「坦白總比欺瞞朋友好得多」。

這首歌曲在一定程度上遵循詩歌對韻腳的要求，以求發音的美感。例如第三段中每句的最後一個單詞有規律的押韻：loud 和 crowd，way 和 say，together 和 forever。

（張旋 譯）

I Have Nothing
一無所有

Share my life, take me for what I am
'Cause I'll never change all my colors for you
Take my love, I'll never ask for too much
Just all that you are, and everything that you do

I don't really need to look very much further
I don't want to have to go where you don't follow
I won't hold it back again
This **passion** inside can't run from myself
There's nowhere to hide
Your love I'll remember

Well, don't make me close one more door
I don't want to hurt anymore
Stay in my arms if you dare
Must I imagine you there
Don't walk away from me
I have nothing, nothing, nothing
If I don't have you

You see through right to the heart of me
You break down my walls with the strength of your love
I never knew love like I've known it with you
Will a memory **survive**
One I can hold on to

**詞彙
註釋**

Don't walk away from me
Don't you dare walk away from me
I have nothing, nothing, nothing
If I don't have you, you...

passion *n.* 激情

survive *v.* 倖存

雲妮‧休斯頓（Whitney Houston）演唱的這首歌是她主演的電影《護花傾情》（*The Bodyguard*）主題曲。這首歌充分體現了雲妮強有力的聲線，尤其是歌曲尾部的連續高音，穿透力非常強勁。

融進我的生活，認識真正的我
我絕不會在你面前掩飾甚麼
請接受我的愛，我並不會要求太多
僅僅是一個本來的你和你所做的一切

我真的不想考慮太多
不想去沒有你陪伴的地方
我不會再壓抑自己的感情
也不會再逃避自己的內心
因為我已無處可逃
我會記住你的愛

不要讓我再次退卻
我並不想傷害任何人
如果你可以，就請抱緊我
我自信你是愛我的
不要離開我
我將一無所有
如果失去了你

你看穿了我的心
你用堅韌的愛擊碎了我的心牆
你讓我明白甚麼是愛
如果記憶可以永存
我會將它緊緊抓住

不要離開我
雖然可以，但請不要
否則我將一無所有
如果失去了你

（劉媛媛 譯）

 精彩之處

這歌歌詞全文體現了電影的劇情發展。歌曲高潮部分 don't make... imagine you there 敘寫蕾切爾對弗蘭克的期待，希望他能勇敢些，擺脫顧慮，共同經營這段愛情；You break down my walls... 道出蕾切爾誤會弗蘭克的真心後，弗蘭克用生命去踐行對她的愛時，她才恍然大悟真愛一直都在。Will a memory survive...nothing 中多次出現 nothing 和 you，將蕾切爾面對為她擋槍倒下的弗蘭克，那種面臨失去至愛時的絕望、悲痛與懊悔表達得淋漓盡致。

Whitney Houston

▶ N O W P L A Y I N G

Saving All My Love for You
我 全 部 的 愛 都 留 給 你

英文
歌詞

A few stolen moments is all that we share
You've got your family, and they need you there
Though I've tried to resist, being last on your list
But no other man's gonna do
So I'm saving all my love for you

It's not very easy, living all alone
My friends try and tell me, find a man of my own
But each time I try, I just break down and cry
'Cause I'd rather be home feeling blue
So I'm saving all my love for you

You used to tell me we'd run away together
Love gives you the right to be free
You said be patient, just wait a little longer
But that's just an old **fantasy**

I've got to get ready, just a few minutes more
Gonna get that old feeling when you walk through
that door
For tonight is the night, for feeling alright
We'll be making love the whole night through
So I'm saving all my love
Yes I'm saving all my love
Yes I'm saving all my love for you
No other woman is gonna love you more

詞彙
註釋

fantasy *n.* 幻想

雲妮·休斯頓被譽為「美國第一嗓」。她一生獲獎 421 次，多首經典歌曲在樂壇創下的紀錄至今無人打破。這首歌收錄在同名專輯中。雲妮的歌唱特點：嗓音強而有力，一字多轉音，音域遼闊。

中文譯文

我們珍惜着這僅有的偷來的時光
你已經有了家庭，家裏人需要你
雖然我試圖離開你
但是沒有人能夠再走進我心裏
所以我會把我全部的愛都留給你

孤獨是一種煎熬
朋友們勸我找個歸宿
但每一次的嘗試都使我崩潰，使我哭泣
因為我寧願待在家裏獨自憂傷
所以我會把我全部的愛都留給你

你曾說我們一起私奔
愛情給予你自由的權利
你說只要耐心等待
但那只是美好的幻想

我已經準備好再次重溫
重溫你
走進我內心深處的感覺
今晚，就今晚重溫吧
我們將整晚沉浸在愛情中
所以我會把我全部的愛都留給你
是的，我會把我全部的愛
是的，我會把我全部的愛都留給你
沒有人比我更愛你

（張玉嬌 譯）

精彩之處

本歌中的男方已經有了自己的家庭，所以女方試圖結束兩人之間的關係，想要重新尋找一份愛，但在尋找過程中卻發現，再也沒有人能夠走進自己的心裏。

door：這裏的 door 一語雙關，既是實指房門，也是虛指「心」門。

歌中 share 和 there，together 和 longer，more 和 door 等兩兩構成押韻，這些以母音構成的尾韻，發音時飽滿到位，給人強烈的震撼。

□ 責任編輯：梁卓倫
□ 裝幀設計：霍明志　李靖琳
□ 排　版：黎品先
□ 印　務：劉漢舉

都是愛情惹的英文歌

□
主編
李音　戴衛平　劉墐

□
出版
非凡出版
香港北角英皇道 499 號北角工業大廈一樓 B
電話：(852) 2137 2338　傳真：(852) 2713 8202
電子郵件：info@chunghwabook.com.hk
網址：http://www.chunghwabook.com.hk

□
發行
香港聯合書刊物流有限公司
香港新界大埔汀麗路 36 號
中華商務印刷大廈 3 字樓
電話：(852) 2150 2100　傳真：(852) 2407 3062
電子郵件：info@suplogistics.com.hk

□
印刷
美雅印刷製本有限公司
香港觀塘榮業街 6 號 海濱工業大廈 4 樓 A 室

□
版次
2016 年 11 月初版
2018 年 1 月第 2 次印刷
© 2016 2018 非凡出版

□
規格
32 開（230 mm×153 mm）

□
ISBN：978-988-8394-53-1

本書原名：《每天讀點英文：經典英文歌曲全集》，
繁體版由中國宇航出版有限責任公司授權出版